Neutral Ground

Marta Jespersen

Copyright © 2014 Marta Jespersen

All rights reserved.

ISBN-13: 978-1496068040
ISBN-10: 1496068041

DEDICATION

To my children: May you always be free thinking and question every known fact.

CONTENTS

Part I	Part II
1 A Wise Man	1 Growing
2 Learning To Cope	2 New Adventures
3 Shaken	3 Traditions
4 After Shock	4 Interruptions
5 Papers	5 Gaining Ground
6 Three's Company	6 New Frontiers
7 Emerging Change	7 Finding Treasures
8 Unrest	8 Loss
9 An End	9 Returning
10 New Beginnings	

Part I

A WISE MAN

It was a bright, sunny August morning, the kind of morning that causes you to stop and stare out the window as you sip on your cup of coffee, listening to the birds. The air was filled with the smells and sounds of a calm summer day—lawn mowers cutting grass, followed by the crisp earthy scent of a freshly planted garden, accompanied by the quiet nagging of a mother bird calling to her chicks; or perhaps that was the neighbour, Mrs. Philips, yelling at the kids to come and eat their breakfast. Of course, I didn't care for all of those fine details as I strolled out of my bedroom—a typical teenaged girls' room plastered in posters of only the sexiest pop stars, and celebrity hunks, clothing strewn across the floor (the debris of trying to decide which mini skirt and tiny top combination to wear to a Friday night party)—and tripped down the stairs, too tired to notice my little brothers' toys lying, like dead soldiers, all over the floor. My father sat, as he did every Saturday morning, at the kitchen table, drinking his coffee, two creams (and God forbid you put sugar in it!), while reading the Weekly Tribune. As I stumbled into the kitchen, hoping that he had made some kind of breakfast, he—in his stoic, Polish way—began "So, how was the party? I hope you didn't embarrass yourself, or the family." And I in my typical, Americanized fashion replied, "It was fine." That is how we left every Friday behind us, and tested the mood of Saturday.

My father was a very wise man, although I would never have admitted it then; I was only fifteen, and too embarrassed to admit to myself, let alone to anyone else, that my father was a great man. His name was Tadeusz, my Babcia, named him after some great Polish hero or another—there were a lot of great Polish men with that name. He was strong, and after the death of my mother he picked up all of the broken pieces, looked at me, and said "Today is a new day, and as we Polish have always done, we'll keep going; we will not give up!" I'm certain he was telling this to himself as much as he was instructing me. So, that's exactly what we did; we kept going. He wasn't a particularly handsome man, at least not by North American standards; but in the Polonia he was well sought after as a bachelor. He was thirty-five when mom died.

And so that perfect Saturday morning continued as it always did. "Tatuniu," I would start, "Did you make anything for breakfast, Maciek is going to be up soon and he'll want to eat."

And of course, as I knew he would, my father would say "No, I didn't make anything. I only ground some coffee." His Polish was smooth, fluid, with the slightest hint of a Canadian accent in his vowels. "Why don't you make us some eggs and sandwiches? Just like mom used to make." I hated him for that; for speaking to me about how mom used to do things, for asking me to take over her role!

"Fine, I guess I can do that." But, something about this morning seemed different to me. He wasn't sitting in his chair, rather he had taken mom's seat—no one has sat there for five years—and he had left the coffee beans out, and the grinder was still sitting on the counter. I started with picking up what he had left behind; something I would learn to do well. When I had finished making breakfast, I walked up the stairs to wake up my brother; he was only six and often called me "Mama".

"Good morning, Maciuszku!" I would sneak into his room, sit down on the edge of the bed, and gently stroke his hair. It never failed; it was an old trick that mom used on me every day. After we ate our breakfast, my brother dressed and went out to play with the neighbour's kids while father and I sat at the kitchen table reading the paper, saying absolutely nothing. That is, until he finished reading the Politics section.

It wasn't until years later that I'd realize just how wise, perhaps clairvoyant, my father actually was. He put down the paper, looked into the air, rubbed his forehead and said "If they don't stop with all this, "Christian" right-winged crap versus "Socialist" left-winged shit soon, and if those damn Americans vote for that woman!" His words grew heavy and thick when he talked about politics "We will never see the end of war! The only end we'll see is a very violent, fiery one!" and at that, my father stood up and left me to finish reading. I always hated Politics. I never understood what was so important about incumbents, left-wing, and right-wing. My father, on the other hand, was very informed. My babcia never let him forget about how difficult communism was, she was always telling stories about waiting in lines that stretched for miles just to get a single loaf of bread and then moving onto the next line to get some meat. It seemed to me that Communism only lead to a lot of waiting, hunger, and alcoholism. But, what did I know? I grew up in the suburbs.

     June 13, my twenty-first birthday. Father had promised to take me to Vegas that year, but as always he had to work. I don't think he ever stopped working, even on the weekends there was something for him to do; a manuscript to read or an article to revise. I never understood why he couldn't take time off to spend with us; he's all we had, and we craved his love. So, instead of taking me he gave me a cheque and told me to go with some friends. I did. I lost everything he gave me, and some of my own money too, but I loved every moment of loss. The whole experience made me feel like I was in some film, or another, waiting for a spy to jump through a window and kidnap me—it was an exhilarating thought. When I came home my father and I didn't have much to say except the usual pleasantries:

"How was Vegas?" he asked

"Fine. I lost it all." I'd reply dryly thinking to myself that I wished he would have been there to share in my losses.

"You didn't do anything shameful, did you?" He would enquire in that patriarchal way.

"No, daddy. How was your week?" and he would go on to tell me about the latest manuscript he'd read, and how terribly it was written. He would then complain that most writers no longer knew how to write, not even in their own language, a language which he had to learn when he was ten. So we sat down and split up the paper, as we did every Saturday. He passed me the Entertainment, Classifieds, and Obits and kept the Business and Politics sections for himself—he knew I didn't care about the Political climate or how the stocks were doing. I didn't even know what stocks were or how they worked; they seemed so arbitrary, false. But, I suppose that is the same with most things.

    My father always told me that he wished I would learn to do something useful; he felt that any career was better than sitting behind a desk organizing someone else's life—I agreed with him, but never really knew what I wanted to do, or what I should do, so I decided to keep sitting behind a desk. I didn't realize until my father had his first stroke why he so desperately wanted me to find a clear path for myself, a good career; he seemed to know before the doctors did that I would have to take care of things.

    It was December 10th, my father's birthday; I was sitting behind my desk preparing a travel itinerary for my boss when I received the call from the hospital:

"Hello, my name is Dr. Richards; I am a neurologist at St. Peter's Hospital. May I please speak with Danuta?" The somber voice asked.

"This is Danuta."

"Yes, Miss, I have some difficult news to share with you. You're father is here, he has had a terrible stroke; I need for you to come and fill out some forms." The good doctor sounded so calm, so resolute, as if nothing had happened, as if my entire world was not about to fall apart.

When I arrived at the hospital, a nurse took me to see him; she handed me the insurance forms and a pen, and told me to fill them out quickly so that she could file them and go home. I hated her for that. I took my father's hand, cried, and asked "What am I going to do now, daddy? Why couldn't you wait? It's only been a year." I cried until I fell asleep.

I remember that day as though it had only happened a minute ago; the day when Maciek went to a friend's house, his first boy-girl party. It was October; the leaves were turning colours and falling softly onto the dying lawns. I had to work late, and father refused to take him—said Maciek was too young for this kind of party—so Maciek walked. It was foggy out that evening; the fog was so thick you could barely see your own hands held out in front of your face. I was in a meeting, taking notes—a skill I had excelled at since middle school—when it happened. Maciek was crossing the street only two blocks from home, when some teenaged moron who had forgotten to turn on his headlights and drove too fast turned the corner. The paramedics said Maciek had died on impact. He was only a month from his twelfth birthday.

When I woke up, I realized that my father's eyes were open; he couldn't speak, the left side of his body was completely paralyzed. My father was only forty-one.
"Tatuniu?" I was surprised to see him awake, and realizing that it was Saturday morning I asked "Would you like me to read you the paper?" My Polish was weak, and my syllables were thick. He nodded. He never liked it when his schedule was interrupted. I ran to the nurses' station to ask for a copy of the

paper, they told me to go to the Cafeteria; I also picked up some coffee and scrambled eggs.

When I started reading to him, I realized what he had said six years before was slowly becoming a reality. What I read terrified me to the very core, and it made me suddenly, peculiarly interested in Politics, and we decided to hold onto the paper for his notebooks. It was an obsession of his, to keep records.

"In tactical response to the threats made by the Chinese Communist government, President Mary-Anne Clark agreed to take the Secretary of Defense's advice and deploy a nuclear bomb to China's capital city, and cultural/economic center—Beijing. The Communist Party has not addressed its people yet, nor have they responded to the attack.

In her State of the Nation address this morning, the President stated "It was the only reasonable way that we could think of to stop the Chinese from spreading their brand of government, their dictatorship, across the globe. The attack on Beijing was not a decision that was made lightly; I urge all American's to take precautions over the coming days. Please ensure your homes are well stocked with non-perishable food items, water, alternative energy sources, and any other items which you may need in the event of a counter-attack." Public outcry against the Government's decision to attack China, as it did Hiroshima and Nagasaki in WWII, seems to resonate even with those who support the attack.

Only hours after the attack took place, crowds began gathering outside of the White House shouting back and forth; Police involvement was heavy, although many claim that even these figures of authority became unruly.

Judy Hall, a 26 year old mother of two, told the Weekly Tribune's Andy Hall, that "even the cops started shouting insults at each other; a few even threatened members of the crowd, and others encouraged those protesting to storm the White House. I had to get myself and my kids out of there!"

The entire American nation, and our neighbours, will wait with bated breath to see what the Chinese government will do in response to our Government's tactics. The Secretary of Defense has issued a public statement concluding that 150,000 American Infantrymen, 100,000 Marines, 120,000 Navy personnel, and an undisclosed number of Air Force personnel will be deployed over the next three days. Air attacks are said to be suspended until further notice, and no other information on Operations will be released to the public. Justin Orynski, Secretary of Defense, stated that "currently there is no reason to implement the Draft. This will only be discussed in the event that we face major retaliation and our military forces require further assistance from our citizens. Although we are not currently enforcing a draft, we do encourage those who are healthy to enlist and help us protect what is rightfully ours!"

--Michael James"

The day I brought father home from the hospital, the sidewalk covered in a foot of snow—I'd been sleeping at the hospital in his room, hoping, praying, that nothing else would happen—was the day that I realized just how right my father had always been. As I watched him try to regain control over his face, wipe his mouth clumsily, and eat sloppily it struck me: he wanted more for me, because he knew that this painful experience was coming. He had always included me when he was done editing a manuscript, he would always ask me what errors he had missed, and I knew he hadn't missed any, he just simply didn't mark them. So I searched the pages (sometimes hundreds, other times only a few), and I picked out the grammatical errors—split infinitives, comma splices, incorrect uses of the semi-colon—and made comments about style and word choice; it was at these moments that my father beamed with pride. He knew that this was what I was meant for, not making coffee and picking up phones, but deciding which novels are worth publishing, which poets ought to be considered and which works of art would stand the test of time.

The day seemed to crawl by, as though every second was drawn out into a minute. After what seemed like an eternity at the dinner table, I drew my father a bath, helped him to wash—the stroke had left him almost incapable of caring for himself, at least until the rehabilitation exercises would start to help, and that wouldn't be for months—dress, and finally I picked up a manuscript that he had left on the table for me to read. It was a common enough story, boy meets girl, boy falls in love with girl and so on; yet, it seemed peculiarly poignant. Perhaps I thought it was a story worth telling in spite of its lacking integrity and its tiredness, or perhaps it was because I wanted a boy to find me, and fall in love with me.

"This house feels so lonely."

The only sentence in that entire book worth mentioning; yet it lacks the depth and emotional charge of anything worth quoting. Perhaps it was poignant because I knew that my house would soon be a very lonely place. I corrected that which my father had left for me to correct, and I wrote a quick note to the author and the publisher:

This story isn't worth the red ink. Try telling something that's worth quoting, perhaps read a little more and write a little less.

D.J.

My father would have been very pleased with the tartness of my address; he would have told me he was proud. But, maybe that's just my illusion, my personal image—a dreamscape—of what my father was. In truth, he rarely spoke about anything except business, politics, and what I should not be doing with my life. I needed him to be a hero, but all I had was a shell of a man.

Three weeks before his stroke, father and I had a fight; I don't think we've ever yelled so loudly at one another before. He was upset that I had put off getting a college degree for so long; he thought I'd never get around to it.

"Kurwa Mac!" he yelled so loud I felt my ears pop "When are you going to decide what you want from your life? What, do you think I'm going to take care of you? That I'll buy you a car, and a house? All that you mother ever wanted for you is to go to University; and all you do is sit on your fucking ass and do nothing!"

"So what?!?" I could yell just as loudly as he could, but my voice would never boom—I would never be able to get his attention like he could get mine—it was too small, and he was such a big man. "Who gives a damn dad? You've always told me to follow my passion, but I don't have any fucking passion! All I have is, well, I don't even fucking know anymore. I've got nothing to offer! Is that what you wanted?" I turned for the door, yanked my purse off the coffee table "I'm leaving. I'll get my shit out of here as soon as I find a place." That was the last time I'd seen him, he was furious, his face was red and sweat gently speckled his forehead—it reminded me of the fights he'd have with mom. A few days before mother died they fought; they'd both been drinking, I remember the stench of Polish beer and vodka in the kitchen and on their sweat—the sweetness of moms perfume mixed with the bitterness of beer and the musk of my father's lightly beaded forehead. They'd been talking about money and my mother suggested that she go out and get a job.

"Danuta is old enough to take care of Maciek when she gets home from school. I can go work in an office. I'm begging you, Tadeusz! Don't be like this!" My mother would plead with him for hours like this, in her soft sing-song kind of way. Even when she was upset or disappointed, she had a way of making you feel comfortable, happy even.

"My wife! God damn it, my wife, will not work! Do you hear me? You will not go to an office asking for a job!" His voice boomed through the entire house and it was at that moment that I became afraid of him. I could never look at him as I had when I was only a little girl. I realized then what I had forgotten so quickly after mother's death: that he was only a fragile man, there was nothing heroic about him; he was weak, even though his voice could penetrate the toughest skin, he remained a small man. It was his pride that made him so small.

As the days passed after father's stroke, I began to realize what I did have. I came to know myself as my father had known me; I had an eye for revisions, I could tell the great stories, the ones that will be told for ages, from those which would be popular for a season, and be quickly forgotten. It's the great ones that academics will show interest in: only those stories which reveal the deepest parts of the human soul make it into the hands of academics, the other ones are good for a quick casual read—like a onetime fuck in an alley behind the bar. It was because he knew what I could do with a book, or a poem, that he pushed so hard, and it was because he couldn't bear to see his wife sulk as she left home to go to work that he pushed her so hard to go get the groceries the evening she died. He knew, and I knew too, that nothing good could ever come of mother going to work, and of me wasting my literary prowess. My father was a wise man after all.

LEARNING TO COPE

Of course I didn't realize that he was my hero until after his death when I was left alone in that big empty house, full of memories, and the lies of unfulfilled dreams. It happened only a few months after he had finished his rehabilitation program, he could finally write, walk, feed himself, and even bathe without my help. I finally felt I could leave him, like I could experience my own life again. I could breathe uninterrupted. His death was sudden; I should have been better prepared. After all, the doctors did warn me that another stroke could happen at any time, especially if he didn't take his meds—which, knowing my father, wasn't a surprising development. I was so angry with him the last time we spoke. He called me at work, pulled me out of an investor's luncheon, simply to tell me that he was fine—he hadn't taken his medication in almost two months—and to lecture me about the monotony of working for an Oil and Gas powerhouse. I yelled at him, told him never to call me at work again, and then I simply hung up. I don't think I'll ever get over those last words.

It should've been me; I'm his daughter, I'm the one who should have found him—I should never have yelled at him! His neighbour, Mr. Melnik, noticed that the newspapers were piling up at the front door and so he decided to check in on my dad. He found him lying on the floor with the phone clutched in his hands; apparently the smell was so bad that Mr. Melnik had to run out of the house before calling for help.

My father was a simple man, and he didn't care for religion, so I had him cremated; I held a small wake at his—our—house and took his ashes to the mountains—it was the only place that he was ever at peace and it seemed like the perfect place to leave him.

When his lawyer called me in to go over the Will I hadn't expected for his last wishes to be so…specific. The major points, house, car, money, were obvious. I was the only one left and it all went to me; but my father knew me, he knew I wouldn't disappoint him after he had died, so he had money set aside for me to go to University so I could become an editor. He had written:

"Dani, you may think it silly, or even selfish of me, but I know that this is the only work that will truly transform you. Stop being so proud, you don't know yourself as I know you; you have a gift and that gift must be shared."

My father did know me, so that Fall I enrolled—although it would prove to be pointless. I seemed to breeze through my classes, the literature wasn't terribly challenging and the professors seemed no better than the hundreds of aspiring writers my father and I turned down time and time again. Perhaps I was over-confident, after all I had been editing—albeit unofficially—for the past eleven years; if I was, then the

Professors didn't seem to care either way. It wasn't until I took my first political science course that I started to engage in my coursework. I could finally understand my father's passion for it. The nuances in political platforms, the basic ideologies that make up the Democratic systems worldwide in comparison to the ideologies of communism and what it really means to be neutral fascinated me. I finally felt challenged, and it showed in my commitment.

Dr. Weitzman, my PoliSci professor, took notice of my coursework—he even began using it to illustrate to the remainder of the class what a good analysis should be, despite my many flawed arguments—and we began meeting outside of the classroom and his office for coffee. It was always the same discussion, of course, the current political climate. We never did allow ourselves to be more than just sounding boards, or that's what we tried to convince ourselves. Dr. Weitzman couldn't risk his career, he didn't want to be one of those professors that are known for their illicit relationships with students—a problem that was once exclusively male centered. There were a number of female professors at the University that were known for their willingness to take sexual favours and bribes in exchange for better grades. Many of them were known to exchange sex for tenure. Although, some professors, to their credit I suppose, would date a student, and go on to get married and start families with them; those were few and far between. We managed to navigate our relationship over tenuous waters. Despite rumours that we were acting against the University charter, we never did. Our relationship remained about Politics until we simply couldn't talk about it anymore, and even then I was no longer his student and the University, well that part can wait.

Dr. Weitzman, Gary, was convinced that the attacks on Beijing, Iran, Iraq, and Mumbai were strategically set two months apart to avoid over exposure of radiation to the atmosphere; I wasn't convinced I'd tell him "Gary, are you kidding? It simply took the Americans that much time to fabricate evidence against these poor, war torn countries, and to convince the American people that it was the right thing to do. You know that the Southern states will almost always go with war when it's proposed as a way to prevent further conflict. Don't you find it convenient that a month after each attack the President claimed that there was no ill doing on the part of the U.S. government? I can't buy that. They slaughtered all of those people and have caused so many more innocents to suffer the aftermath!" He'd always smile at me, as if I had finally caught on to the most important principle in Politics—trust nothing that the government claims as truth. "Oh, Dani," he'd say sweetly "this is exactly why you're my favourite pupil." And he'd lean over the table, take my face in his hands and gently—almost paternally—kiss my forehead.

Of course I couldn't tell anyone about our unofficial meetings; our secret weekends at the cabin became a source of anxiety between us, even though we weren't doing anything that was against University regulations—there was never anything illicit about our relationship, my grades were never affected by our relationship, and our discussions and getaways were always prompted by Politics. Gary and I were friends.

He made it very clear that a sexual relationship between us was impossible; he couldn't risk his entire career, nor could I risk disappointing my father—even in his death father's voice rang clear with every decision I made.

    It bothered Gary that I had such a hard time letting go of my Father, but then again Gary's father was a figment of his imagination—a phantom he invented as a child. In truth, Gary's father never even knew he had a son. His mother met him at a bar—she claimed she drank too much that night—and went back to his apartment; she never saw him again. I believe her though; she has a tendency of drinking too much. It kills me to see how broken he is whenever his mother visits. I wish I could save him from his pain, just as I wish I could've saved my father from Mother's death and my brother from that car. I felt helpless. It's always been in my nature to take care of others, perhaps it's because of how mother was. She never let us do anything that would cause us any harm, real or perceived. Even watching us clean our rooms seemed too difficult for her; perhaps she thought that the only way to justify staying home and letting father work so hard was to do all of the domestic duties, even the ones that as children we wanted to do. We never complained about cleaning up after ourselves, and we were always happy to help her—I saw how worn and tired she looked, and how her hands cracked from the dry prairie air and constant exposure to suds. Father used to tell me how mother would smile with her eyes, even when she was wearing a frown, or mourning the loss of a neighbourhood friend; but he didn't notice when her eyes stopped smiling. When mother got sick, her eyes grew faint; she became pale and tired looking. Her body started to wilt; the woman I had seen love with every fibre of her being slowly began to fade. Her body became emaciated and her soul—the fire that my father loved so much—died months before her body was ready to give up. Gary, on the other hand, had only seen his mother smile on select occasions; his fondest memories of her were the times that she wasn't drunk. She'd sobered up a few times, but it never stuck. On her final visit with Gary she looked at him, with her sad, sunken eyes and said "Baby, don't you ever be like your momma! You hear? You make sure that you always deal honest, and tha' you make right by tha' girl. I'm sorry I couldn't ha' been betta at motherin' you. You're a good boy, you always has been. I love you, son. You remember that, won't you?" It took every fibre of his being to answer his mother, but he did "Don't worry momma, I won't forget. I love you too. Now let's get you in that cab so you can get home." As soon as his mother left, we both knew what was coming. She'd never apologized for her absence before.

"You know Dani," Gary laughed "you need to stop worrying about me so much. I'm a grown man, and can take care of myself." He said, unconvincingly.

"I can't help it, Gary. I care too much about you to let you hurt like this." I wanted to tell him everything. How it killed me every time he'd kiss my forehead, or how broken I felt after a weekend at the cabin, knowing that I couldn't have him in every way I needed him. That it took every bit of my strength to not break down when he left my apartment in the middle of the night, smelling of wine and cigars.

"Dani," he looked at me sheepishly, like a little boy looking for his mother's approval "I can't do this to you anymore. You used to have so much fight, but now it's as though you're struggling to breathe. Please," he gently lifted my face to meet his eyes, tears starting to well up in his, "tell me whatever it is you need to say. You've been holding back your words for months."

"I can't do that, Gary. If I do, then we won't be able to do this anymore. It'll become too complicated and too hard for both of us."

"Don't you think it's been hard for me too? Do you really think that I plan these weekends simply because we're good friends? Or because you're my best student? Don't you think I want more?" He'd never yelled before. It frightened me. "I'm sorry, I didn't mean to yell. It's just that I've been trying for so long not to say these things. I've been a coward, I, I...."

"Shut up, Gary." I placed my finger over his lips, hushing him "You've never been great with words." I turned away from him so that he couldn't see the tears welling up. "Now," deep breath "I'm gonna go pack up the rest of the food, and get everything ready for the weekend. Can you run to the store and grab some bug spray; we ran out last weekend."

"Sure." As he climbed into the car I walked, slowly, carefully, and controlled back inside the apartment building and for the first time since father's death, I cried. I knew that everything had changed the second he showed up on the front step; I had planned this after all. It was weak of me to assume that we could have it all; in fact it was just foolish. I knew that his career was everything to him, and I knew that until I graduated he would never be able to move past the student-teacher dynamic, but I had to try. I just needed to release it all, knowing that nothing could happen, and that our friendship would fizzle out like the campfire did when we stayed up too late, drinking, and trying not to touch.

There's an old adage that couples often use when they're talking about adultery: You can look, but you can't touch. Well, that was our unspoken philosophy regarding each other, we looked, we desired, we even dreamt about it—at least I did—but we never dared to draw too close, and if ever we had the slightest shimmer of a moment we pulled away quickly. It was our pact: to never touch. But hope, it would seem, never leaves the minds of the stubborn; and if Gary knew me at all, he knew that stubbornness was my best quality. He never did come back that day, but he did call to tell me that this weekend couldn't happen; there was too much tension. So, I decided to go to him; and it was on that night that the world began coming undone.

Gary and I had always talked about it, usually in passing. He had read that same article that I had read to my father in the hospital. We knew that one day China would strike back against the Americans for that attack. They left millions for dead, for months there were reports of radiation clouds wafting towards the coast off British Colombia and California, but the Canadian Health Minister ensured us that we were safe in Alberta, so we never really worried about it much. It was about 6:00 pm when I made it to Gary's. When I walked in I saw him standing in the middle of his living room, a glass shattered on the floor, the red wine seeping—creeping almost—towards the white throw rug which softened the hardwood floor; the spot which we always cleared for intimate discussions about Kant and Sartre, sometimes inviting Nietzsche into our little circle, was covered in newspaper clippings and file folders.

"Gary?" I hesitated, lingered in the doorway for a few more seconds and that's when I saw it—the image of downtown Manhattan covered in flames, the screams of thousands, no hundreds of thousands of souls as they burned, trying to escape. I inched towards him, and before I knew it I was standing next to him clutching his hand "Was it..?" "Yeah. It just happened." Gary softly wrapped his arm around my shoulders "They think it was China." I could feel my knees buckle. My mind told me that this was impossible, and my body told me to run, to hide. I knew that I would never do that; it was too important to stay now, to push myself to find a way to survive what was surely to come next.

"We should go to the cabin, Dani. We could live there if shit gets bad here." Those blue eyes looked at me, worried, afraid, alone.

"It won't get bad, Gary. Everything's changed."

SHAKEN

I didn't get home until late Sunday. Gary and I had stayed up all night on Saturday watching the news, going over old newspaper clippings and government files which had been made public. I hadn't realized how far gone his obsession was with that bombing, he had only said "They didn't toss that nuke at China for no reason; it's too risky a move." I had known he was researching Canadian ties to Chinese officials, and trade operations between China, Canada and the U.S.; but I hadn't realized that the reason he had wanted to go to the cabin was because he knew it was coming, and he wanted to protect me from it. By Sunday night the U.S.

had openly declared war on China. The Middle East joined forces with China, bringing sanctions against the U.S. and Canada—no imports or exports, and all Canadians, Americans or Europeans left on Middle Eastern or Asian soil after Monday would be hunted like wild animals, and killed. Mohammed Assaraf, the Iranian president, had given them just enough time to have hope that they could make it home, but on Monday at 1:00 am his troops stormed the airports taking no prisoners.

"This is it, Gary. There's no escaping this war, no negotiating, no talks; all that's left to do is slaughter." I had said that after the initial broadcast was over, and we drank our warm beer and snacked on Triscuits and Havarti. I couldn't imagine what would come next. "Who do you think is going to join the war next? Canada?" Gary looked at me, knowing that if Canada did enter in we'd probably get drafted within months. "We can't leave. How will we know what's going on if we go?" All I wanted to do was lie there with my head in his lap, and shut out the thoughts of death, destruction and nuclear bombs. "I know, but at least we can stop pretending. I won't be teaching much longer, not if this war goes any further." His timing couldn't have been worse; the last thing I wanted at that moment was a relationship, I needed to focus on what to do next to survive. "The kit, Gary!" He looked at me puzzled "Our camping kit! We always have enough food, water, and toiletries to last us weeks, months if we ration it out." His eyes softened, "Yeah, but it's all at the cabin, at least all the tinned foods. Should we drive down tomorrow and gather it all up and bring it here?" He pulled his arms around me, embracing me from behind "Maybe we can take the week out there to gather our thoughts, figure out all of our "what ifs". We have the satellite out there so we can watch the news to stay updated." He kissed my neck softly. "Gary," I pleaded "We can't do this now. Tomorrow we'll need to go to the grocery and hardware stores; we'll get fresh produce and we can stock up on frozen meats and vegetables. Get enough to last us a month, at least. We'll need to get some seeds or seedlings from the hardware store, some fertilizer, gardening supplies; we can plant a garden for ourselves at the cabin." I pried his arms off of me and walked to the kitchen, had a drink of water, and lied down in bed.

"Dani," Gary whispered and gently shook me "Dani, wake up. I made you some breakfast. I hope you don't mind, but I stayed with you last night; you were having some really violent dreams and I didn't want to leave you like that." He brushed my hair from my eyes and kissed my forehead. This time it was different, this time it wasn't a purposeful kiss to avoid my lips, it was meant to comfort me; I didn't want to be comforted. "Get in here!" I said pulling him into bed. It wasn't what I had planned our first time together to be, it was spontaneous; it was free. We were free.

After breakfast, we watched the news again; hoping, praying, that it had all been our imaginations. We never did make it to the grocery store, nor to the hardware store. We stayed in bed for most of the afternoon, making up for hundreds of awkward pauses, and unfulfilled kisses. We knew that if we went to the store on Monday, most foods would be picked through; Sunday was a very violent day. Stores started handing out food for free, not because it was the right thing to do, but because the employees were scared and only wanted to make it home alive, and with some way to feed their families. Electronics stores were ransacked; jeweler's pilfered for any item of value— great or small. Firearms sales were up 400% in the days following the attack on Manhattan—all this in Canada, I could only imagine the panic in American homes; everyone knew that no one could stop what was coming. All Gary and I could do was sit, and wait.

We received the e-mail from the University's president on Monday morning. All classes were cancelled; the University was shutting down for the foreseeable future. Gary and I decided to go there, grab some books, research, and files out of his office. That's when we saw them, soldiers casing the University halls, searching offices for records, research, books, whatever they could find that might give them some insight into what's going on. "You there!" one of them called out to us "Stop what you're doing; all papers, research, notes, books, articles are now the property of the Government of Canada. You are impeding on a Federal investigation." Gary and I looked at each other; we instinctively knew what the other was thinking. "Run?" I mouthed. "Just grab that folder from the desk first; it's my latest research." Gary whispered. I shoved the folder into my purse; as soon as I pulled my hand away from the clasp I heard the screams. "Was that? Iza?!?" I looked at Gary, puzzled, afraid. "Run! Gary! They want your research! They'll..." BANG, Iza's body fell to the floor at the end of the dim hallway; I couldn't move. "Run, Dani! GO!!!!" It was as though my body and my mind weren't connected for the first few steps, and finally everything made perfect sense. We ran through the marble halls, down the five flights of stairs and out to the car. As we stepped out into the sunlight we heard the shouting and gunfire. "Stop! Arrete!" We knew that nothing good could happen now. So we drove without stopping. When we pulled up in front of Gary's apartment building we noticed the shadows moving around in his bedroom "It's a good thing I don't go anywhere without my files; they won't find anything there. We need to go to the cabin; before they see us sitting here."

"Gary, what exactly have you been researching? And why the fuck is the Canadian military ransacking your apartment? Please, if we're going to do this together then I need to know everything!" I looked across from the passenger's seat at him, knowing deep down in my heart, that the only reason he never kissed me before was to protect me from all of this; it was never because of his being a professor, he knew the war was coming, and he knew that both sides would want him, would torture him, and he couldn't hurt me like that. But now it's different, maybe it's because he figured they'd want me just as much because they would assume that he would have told me everything, that we were romantically involved. We did spend an awful lot of time together, alone. "Stop staring at me, and read what's in the folder you took. That's what they wanted." Gary staid his gaze at the road ahead of him; I looked through all of the papers—hacked information off of Canadian, U.S., Iranian, and Chinese classified databases, names, dates, Black Ops, everything that the military wants secret. This was Information that could mean all the difference between winning and losing the War; between falling into a pile of ash, and taking power over the developed world.

      We stopped at the gas station, and used the ATM to take out all of our cash, took cash advances off of our Credit Cards, filled up and stocked up on protein bars and beef jerky. We knew that we would never be able to come back. I would never have the chance to sit in on one of Gary's lectures, or to walk the hallowed halls of McGill again. I knew from the moment I stepped through the doors of the Airport into the stench of gasoline and the sounds of Airport Shuttles and taxis that I could never go back to Alberta; to the quiet streets of small towns and the still air of a hot prairie summer. Montreal had me in her grasp, and she would never let go. It wasn't until I realized that I would never walk through the historic plazas or sip coffee and rip croissants that I finally understood what was awaiting me. I loved the cabin and the woods, I loved the smell of the forest floor in early autumn, and I loved that the cabin now held endless possibilities for me and Gary; it was our Eden, and we had not tasted of its forbidden fruits, yet.

"We need to stop in Domaine-des-Rentiers to throw off the search." Gary said quietly.

"Huh? I didn't catch that." I looked at him surprised, shaken out of my thoughts, my short memories of a place that I've called home for only a year; a place where I felt I had belonged for the first time.

"I said, we need to stop somewhere away from our normal route, Domaine-des-Rentiers is the closest and won't set us too far off course, but if we make small talk with someone at a café or shop we'll throw the cops off of our true course." He looked at me annoyed, puzzled. It was as though he blamed me for what happened back at his office.

"Gary," I started my voice shaky and lacking the confidence I needed to tell him my fears "will they find us? What are we going to do all the way out there? And, how in the HELL did you get your hands on these files?!?" My voice rose and fell melodically with the first two questions, but with the last it was as though all of my frustrations, fears, puzzlement, all of me burst out of my throat to strangle the man that brought this new, unexpected twist into my life. I wasn't sure that love would sustain us for very long. We were both too passionate.

"We'll be fine, Dani. No matter what happens next we'll be alright. We're Canadian...how bad can it be?" He peaked over at me, and his eyes betrayed his fear.

My Uncle had been in the Canadian army; he never talked about it. Whenever I would climb up onto his lap and ask him about his experiences overseas, about the missions, the people, the friends he lost he would always snap "You know I can't talk about that! It's all confidential." His eyes would fall to the ground, and he would gnaw on his bottom lip while tears welled up in his eyes. My father would take me from my Uncle's lap into the kitchen; he would seat me on a stool, look me straight in the eyes and say "Oh, oh, oh, what have you done! Dani, you know you're Uncle can't talk about the army! Tsk tsk tsk" My father would shake his head, his brow furrowed in an attempt to decipher how he could bring his little brother back. I didn't understand my Uncle's reluctance to talk about it until I started learning about Post Traumatic Stress Disorder, and about the unclassified missions—particularly the ones that my Uncle had a key role in orchestrating. When I learned how many thousands of children died as a result of one of his plans in Afghanistan 2009, I could no longer remember him the same; and I understood his tears and the rawness of his lips.

   Gary and I drove silently the rest of the way to Domaine. When we arrived we stopped in at a local café, sat down for a latte and crème puffs and made a point to talk with our waitress about where we were headed. We told her we were going up North to Nunavut in hopes of seeing some of the dying wildlife—the Polar Bear was all but extinct at this point, and the arctic ice had receded to a tenth of what it had been in 2012. Our waitress's name was Emilie, she was beautiful, and I couldn't understand why she would stay in such a small town. She could have been very successful in Hollywood. My father would have criticized her harshly for wasting her beautiful face on dirty dishes and washcloths. Then again, my father criticized everyone harshly, even himself. He knew very well what his strengths were and he knew that he had only half of the patience that my mother had. I was too much like my father, and it frightened me. What if the woods couldn't contain my passion? What if Gary became irritating? What if it wasn't enough? When we left that café we knew that we would be safe for some time. We drove through the night until we got to the cabin; Gary suggested we take turns driving. I went first; we both knew that by midnight I'd be asleep at the wheel, and that I couldn't sleep until dark anyways. When we got to the cabin the sun was just beginning to rise, and it painted the sky all shades of pink and orange, and for a moment it felt as though I was back in Alberta. I felt safe.

We unpacked the car, and got ourselves set up in the Cabin; everything had its place, and we knew we could survive here for months if necessary. Gary went up onto the roof of the cabin and set up the satellite—

he had rigged it so that we could get all of the major news networks for free. I never did understand why he would bother bringing a satellite dish and a television out here; I never thought it would be something indispensible to us. While he hooked up the television—an old device from the early 1990's, and the only good thing his father had left—I prepped our breakfast and set the table. The weather was nice so we could air out the sheets and open up all of the windows. We knew that the cleaning and prettying up the cabin should only take us a half day, but we did everything we could to make it last until we'd need to go to sleep. Neither of us wanted to talk about the events from the past couple of days.

That night, the image of Iza's lifeless body hitting the floor haunted me; after the third nightmare I was determined not to sleep, so I picked up the files that we managed to recover from the apartment and the office and started sorting them according to Country, date, and operation/class type. It took me all night, but by the time the sun rose and Gary came out of the bedroom the files were ready to review, discuss and help us to understand why Iza had to die, and why the American's bombed Beijing.

"You look like shit." Gary intoned nonchalantly.

"You're an ass." I retorted "I couldn't sleep so I thought I'd sort files; I do have years of experience doing that, you know." Gary smiled at me; that smile where only the right corner of his mouth lifts and he drops his chin into the palm of his left hand.

"And here I thought you were about to say something mean. Coffee?" He turned towards the coffee maker.

"Definitely! I suppose I don't need to ask you how you slept, since I heard you snoring up a storm in there." I glanced in his direction, his arms were pressing into the wood countertop whilst his body slouched down—I knew he had dreamt of Iza's death, I heard his yells to the dream. It would be a memory that would haunt us both, that would keep us focused.

As soon as the coffee was ready we started fingering through the papers, trying to put together the puzzle. We were prepared to work for months on this; it wasn't uncommon for us to work on one of Gary's research projects at the Cabin, in fact, we preferred it to the clustered office at McGill. We cleared the furniture to the outer edges of the common room and spread the files out in linear order. When the files were all sorted and lain out I swallowed hard, looked at Gary and before I could even begin forming the words in my mouth he stood up, and brushing his jet black hair back with his long, slender fingers began to tell me about how he stumbled upon these documents.

"Don't ask. Okay? Just let me tell you without the pressure of your asking me. I know I have to tell you where all of these came from, how I got them, and why. I get that; I really do, Dani. It's just that" he paused, taking a long, deep breath and turning on his heels as he paced frantically, waving his hands around in some pathetic attempt at sign language "I don't want you to hate me. I never meant for you to get pulled into this; this was never meant for you. I've been at this for a long time, and I have thousands more files just like this. I swear, I'm not a spy or anything like that. I just, well" deep breath "I don't really know what I am."

"Gary," I began, standing up from my criss-crossed position on the hardwood floor, my feet tingling with the renewed sensation of blood rushing through them. My eyes looking up to meet his "I don't need to know any of this. We'll just pretend that this is another weekend at the cabin going through research and cross-referencing the significant passages. We'll shut off the TV. and just focus on this. We can act as if none of that happened." He put his arms around my waist, his hands pressing against my back, and he kissed my forehead.

"If only it were that simple." His voice was weak, breathy, as though he'd just been punched in the stomach, and his piercing blue eyes shifted to that shade of grey painters use to denote melancholy. His heart seemed to sink, and his face betrayed his guilt. "You need to know. If you don't then I won't be able to convince you that we can never go back. Not to Montreal, not to McGill; we're stuck here, and we'll only be able to communicate with my contacts." His eyes searched my face as I sunk back down to the floor, squatting with my elbows on my knees and my face buried in my hands. "Well," I began "I suppose it's a good thing I don't have anyone that loves me out there. Start talking; at least it'll keep me entertained for a while. Lunch?" I got up off of the floor, and slowly walked towards the kitchen; breathless with panic, I kept my composure.

    He told me every detail; how he'd been sent the first files on China in 2025, three years before we met. He explained that he never knew when the next files would come, or who sent them; all he had was an e-mail address, and he was certain that it wasn't traceable. The first files gave him instructions to: "Work through the holes, not beyond them. Make contact when you're done. We will send more." The note was initialed N.G.; Gary gave the initials the name "Neutral Ground" when they started sending files not just on China, but on the U.S. and Canada too. The latest set of instructions was for him to burn everything, and to watch the news in the coming days, but he couldn't burn the files; he wanted to be certain that his predictions were correct.

"So, why?" I asked him, as though it was just another one of his lectures on Plato or Aristotle. "Why what, Dani? Why did the Americans nuke Beijing? Who the fuck knows; I sure as hell don't. Nothing in the U.S. files tells why they did it; at least I couldn't find anything. Maybe I de-coded it incorrectly. That's why we need to go through it all again!" At this point he was yelling again, his brow was furrowed and the sweat was starting to bead on his forehead.

"Okay, let's take a break. We can watch the latest news to see what's happening out there, have some dinner, and just take the night off." I tried to calm him down, but he was too worked up. "No, we can't stop now." His gaze dropped to the floor, like a small child's when its mother is upset.

AFTER SHOCK

It took us a few weeks to get settled into a routine; after four days of non-stop research Gary fell asleep in the middle of a file. He had all of the pages laid out around him, and sat in the centre of it with a cup of iced coffee. I was in the bathroom washing away the pen and pencil marks off of my face from that night's research session. When he screamed I ran out of the bathroom, my face and hands still covered in the gentle scrubbing cleanser. "Are you ok? What happened?" I was short of breath, the adrenaline pumped through me with the simple thought that we had been caught.

"I dozed off with a cup of iced coffee, and now all of the papers are fucking ruined!" Gary turned around with his arms outstretched pointing to the file that he had encircled himself in, and when he finally turned towards me we both started laughing; I at his coffee stained pants, and he at my soapy face, wet hair, and rag doll clothes.

"You look like a mess, Dani!" he chortled "Why don't you finish getting washed up and help me hang these papers on the line outside."

"Sure." I drew a breath in as though I was just coming back from a drowning—an event which haunts me from childhood. I was only seven when it happened. It was my very first swimming lesson—my parents couldn't afford to put me in organized sports, swimming lessons and all of that nonsense that other kids did, so the first time I stepped into a pool was in first grade with all of my other classmates who had been taking lessons since they were six months old—and even though the instructor had put me in a lifejacket, when she encouraged me to go down the slide I inhaled the water just as my head dipped under for that split second. I was taken to the hospital because I had become unconscious and unresponsive, needless to say my parents refused to allow me to take swimming lessons through the school again.

When I was finished with washing up, and felt ready to tackle the day, I walked out onto the porch, the sun peeking in through the trees surrounding us, the smell of fresh forest air hitting every inch of me, cleansing me of all my years spent breathing the smog of big Canadian cities, when my eyes focused in on Gary standing at the line pinning 8"x11" sheets of illegally obtained Chinese documents in hopes that his coffee spill didn't wipe away any pertinent information.

"Well, you clean up nice!" Only his eyes moved towards me, the rest of him was hell bent on getting these papers dry and ready. As I walked towards him and his papers, the generator which had been powering our cabin caught my eye and I couldn't help but wonder how many more hours of electricity we had left.

"Hey, do you know how much fuel we have left in that generator?" I asked him.

"I just checked it last night, and it's at about half, and I've got another three tankfulls worth of fuel in the cellar." He looked at me puzzled "Why?"

"Oh, I just thought that we should be a little more careful with how much we use. Maybe we should stop using the electrical appliances, and save the generator for fueling our lights at night, and the television so we can keep up on what's going on back home." I passed him another clothespin.

"Yeah. You're probably right. Ummm I've got this if you can clean up the floor inside so it doesn't get sticky." He quickly glanced at me, then back to his task.

"Sure. Hungry?"

"I could eat." So we left the chaos of that morning behind us with toast, and eggs. We ate our breakfast quickly and quietly, not because we didn't have tons to talk about, but because there were things we avoided discussing. Gary wasn't sure how to label our relationship, and I didn't want to label it, I'd soon be out of birth control, and going to see a doctor was out of the question—we were fugitives after all. We did what we did every morning after breakfast; we turned on the generator and watched the news for an hour, but what we saw and heard shocked us almost as much as watching Manhattan burn. Manhattan had, of course, been quarantined—no one was allowed to leave the island unless they had entered after the attack in full Hazmat gear. I used to laugh whenever I saw actors suited up in what looked like giant yellow rubber gloves with a plastic face shield on television shows; the real Hazmat suits are little more ominous than that, not because they look that different, but because there is a reason for wearing them.

The anchor on the news was announcing that there had been a Nuclear threat uttered against the U.S. and Canada by Russia, and as an attempt to deter further action by the Russian government, and as a sign of goodwill and support towards Canada and the U.S., all armed NATO countries were preparing their stored missiles, and Canada would place its own weapons on Standby. The Prime Minister was scheduled to make a public service announcement during the evening news. Neither one of us was prepared for what was coming.

After the morning broadcast we turned off the generator, opened up all of the windows, it was a balmy day, the first of many, and the cabin was quickly becoming too hot for us to work efficiently. We decided, after only a couple of hours of searching through the pages that Gary didn't bathe in his iced coffee, to take a break and go for a swim in the creek to cool off. The walk to the creek always revived me more than the swim did, perhaps it was the time spent away from looking at pages, hoping to have that "Eureka!" moment, and to be able to explain everything that had happened in the past year, but that moment never seemed to come. There was nothing in the American documents that suggested any reason for bombing Beijing, and it's obvious that Beijing sent a nuke out of retaliation; Russia's growing involvement wasn't surprising, they had always supported Communist regimes in efforts to bring down the Capitalist pigs. As for myself, I wasn't sure who the bad guys were anymore. Even just a few weeks prior I would have sided with the U.S., they're Canada's neighbor, and they're a Democratic nation—or so it seemed. But then, the more I waded through their confidential documents, the more I got to understand what that nation stood for, the more I questioned Capitalism and its merits. I'd read all of the great thinkers on democracy, and on free trade, but there was nothing free about the U.S. markets. They had created a bottleneck for themselves back in 2005—I was still a fairly young girl, but I remember watching the news with my father and cowering at the images of President George W. Bush Jr.

All of the files that Gary passed me had to do with Bush's administration. It was corrupt to the core. Bush had been nothing more than a puppet for the GOP, the richest television preachers pretty well owned him, and shared him with the oil barons. I knew that in 2002 when he sent troops into Afghanistan and Iraq that the U.S. wouldn't leave until every last drop of oil belonged to them; and they sat there in those deserts, until there was no one left to stand in their way. The most convincing file was the one titled "Operation Alpha and Omega". The name itself stirred up something deep down, it took me five minutes just to look past it and start looking at the content.

Operation Alpha and Omega was drafted in 2004; it detailed the progression of the war on terror. It went back to the 9/11 attacks—referencing Operation Dooms Day, a government planned attack on its own citizens in hopes to blame a religious group in Afghanistan called the Al Qaeda, where they had planted a CIA trained agent to act as the leader and make threats against the United States; this would be their reasoning for declaring war, on a nation that neighbours some of the greatest stores of oil in the Eastern hemisphere. Bush was the perfect president for these attacks, after all he was the son of the man who marched the U.S. troops into the Gulf War; he would simply be finishing what his father had started, and for Americans that would be enough—Revenge is always a great motivator for patriotism. Operation Alpha and Omega went on to describe how Bin Laden would be extracted, and hidden from the rest of the world, and a lay person would be put in his place to be killed as part of the mission to find and eliminate the supposed terrorist responsible for the deaths of thousands of Americans. The Operation also detailed minor missions, infiltrations on small villages that were "key" to the Al Qaeda effort, propaganda messages to be filtered into the media during the 2008, 2012, and 2016 election seasons, and the bombing on Beijing, but there are papers missing, pieces of the puzzle that aren't there. The file ends abruptly with "Target X: a nuclear deterrent will be launched at 1200 hours EST from the USS Bainsbridge Destroyer to make impact at approximately 1400 hours EST. All diplomatic methods must fail for complete success."

    The water in the creek was ice cold on our hot, sweaty skin; we had cooped ourselves up in the cabin for the past week, and the walk through the heavy brush, bright with colour and saturated with smell was a welcome reprieve from the dim light and dank air of the cabin, but no matter how far away from the cabin we were to go, our minds would always go back there, to the files and the hope of finding answers and exposing some sort of truth. We decided to make the most of our time away from the cabin, and set up some rabbit snares and picked some wild berries and mushrooms; I let Gary take the lead on the mushrooms, because although my father spoke fondly of going mushroom hunting with his mother when he was a boy in Poland, he never ventured to take me and my brother out to the woods. He would always say things like "The woods here are different, the mushrooms won't taste very good anyways." I think he was just too scared to relive those memories, because when he and his mother got home, he knew that they would find his father on the sofa with a half empty bottle of Vodka, and a mean temper. The woods in Poland were his peaceful place, and he couldn't bear to go somewhere else and find peace.

    We spent the afternoon hiking, swimming, gathering, and making love. We were running low on fresh food, and we wanted to leave as much of our canned fruits and vegetables as possible for winter, which was still months away. The Indian summer was refreshing, and it would allow us to keep our supplies high for the long winter months that were coming. By the time we had gone back to the cabin it was close to supper hour, so we skinned, gutted, and cooked the two rabbits we had snared over a fire, cleaned and sautéed the mushrooms we had found and made a salad out of all sorts of weeds that we knew were safe. It would take time to get used to this kind of existence, but although we didn't know it then, we would have another year of this to look forward to.

"That was a nice break. It felt like we were just out here camping." Gary looked at me from across the table "I miss that."

"Me too. Oh, that reminds me, we should grab those papers off the line. It looks like rain." I couldn't bear to talk about what we used to do, about the hours we'd spend in the creek never touching, always fearing that if we did Gary would lose his position at the University. We quickly took the papers off the line, they were dry—stained, but none of the ink had faded, so the pages were still easy to read. When we turned on the generator so we could watch the Prime Minister address the nation's concerns we decided to pull out what we did have from the CSIS, and Canadian Military. As we waded through the countless useless files stating that Canada would remain neutral on American involvement in minor operations, the PM's address started.

"Tonight, I greet you with a heavy heart," after eight years of campaigning and nominations Amanda LaBeque had finally won the Liberal leadership race two years prior to the attack on Beijing, and less than a year later, when news had leaked about severe corruption in the Conservative Cabinet—bribes, corporate conflicts of interest, robo-calling, etc.—she won the seat of Prime Minister, "today I regretfully must state that as our national security is closely linked with that of our neighbours, we must hold sanctions against the actions of the Chinese government, and that of Russia and any other communist nation. Travel abroad will be prohibited to all non-democratic nations, and Corporations will pull all manufacturing out of China immediately. If Communist leaders, and those countries which support communist threats of global decimation of Democracy and Capitalism, do not immediately cease their acts of aggression, we will follow our friends in the United States of America into battle. Canada was founded on the principles of free enterprise, and our Constitution requires that we protect our Democratic System. Furthermore, in the interest of safety and continued order, I have ordered the Canadian Military, with the help of private contractors, to step in and aid the RCMP in enforcing law. The courts are officially dismissed in a cost-saving measure, and sentencing for crimes will be up to the discretion of each operational head. Each municipality will be awarded an operational centre. The threats against our great country are real, and unparalleled. We must take every precaution necessary to keep our sovereignty intact." Her voice was monotone, and heavy. After reiterating her speech in French, LaBeque stepped down from the podium and the press was informed that she would not be taking any questions at the time—she was found dead the next morning, and marshall law was declared.

"Well, that was interesting" I could see that Gary was starting to make connections between our

Canadian and American files. "Grab everything we have on Alpha and Omega, and any corresponding Canadian files from around the same time. I think I remember some corresponding language." The look on his face was intense, his brow was furrowed, his eyes darted back and forth as though he were already scanning the pages, his entire body was stiff, and his breathing was rapid. I knew he was having one of those brilliant moments—much like the one that made me realize that there was more to this PoliSci professor than tweed jackets, and coffee stained shirts. I brought him the files, and we flipped through them like mad; seconds meant connections made or missed because in that inspired moment of thought, the brain connects things that normally would seem to be on different paths.

"Here!" he jumped up with two pieces of paper in his hands. He ran them over to the kitchen table, where I was sitting, quietly sipping on a cup of tea, and waiting for his "Eureka!" moment. It didn't take him long to figure out which pages he needed, they were the exact same page from the two separate dockets. "I can't believe I missed these!" He was panting, I could tell his entire body was on fire with excitement; his pupils were dilated, nostrils flared and every muscle tense.

"This is it, babe! This is the breakthrough we needed!" He grabbed the sides of my head and kissed me violently "We should look for similar phrasing in all of the Western files that we have, and corresponding phrasing in the Easter files as well." I got up from the kitchen table and took the three steps towards the kitchen in what seemed like slow motion. My heart was pushing against my chest, and my breathing became shallow with the realization that somehow Canada was involved in one of the greatest conspiracies of our time. "I always thought that our country was about re-building, and helping to establish peace in war torn countries. How? Why?"

"Dani, The U.S. essentially owns Canada. It's in our country's interest to seem unbiased, and unwilling to wage wars, but still remain sided with the States." He put his hand gently on my shoulder. "We should have a snack and get to work to see if we can find more connections."

"Yeah. I'll get the pot on for tea, if you could grab the berries we picked earlier."

"Sure."

That's how we left my bewilderment; unsolved, still burning and questioning. I think it's how he wanted me to feel—he had always disliked my views on Canada's politics, and I suppose he had always been right to.

PAPERS

"So?" I looked at Gary, "what does it say?"

"Read it yourself." He tossed me the pages "I'm going to start looking through the Eastern files. With the amount of stuff we've found between the North American, and European documents, I'm convinced there has to be something on the other end of the spectrum. Why else would our anonymous source send us all of these files?"

The question was rhetorical, of course, but I couldn't help but remind him that these files were his, and I was just an innocent bystander that couldn't help but join in his search out of curiosity. It made him laugh—his first laugh in four days.

Project Alpha and Omega discussed the

conspiracy to provide the public with reasonable cause to invade Oil Rich Iraq, providing a religious group as a scapegoat, and went on to suggest the need to rid the face of the earth of "The Red banner". The Canadian Military's corresponding document: Mission #00200590011 stated "In the event that friendly forces instigate Projects for the capture and seizure of foreign liquid assets, deny all involvement, but proceed to rally citizens in favour of war effort. Enter designation Alfalfa/Irene in support of protection of democracy. Continue fiscal and military efforts to support decimation of enemy forces." Alongside this, the Canadian Security Intelligence Service document regarding the bombing of Beijing, Project Kingpin, showed us that it was Canada's nukes that hit the Chinese centre. The blood of millions of Chinese men, women, and children, and the lives of thousands of tourists were lost because of Canada's policy to support the U.S. in all military activity. The project was designed to anger Communist nations worldwide, in order to provide the U.S. with just cause to go on the offensive, while keeping Canada's international image of a peaceful nation.

I had to wonder if the Prime Minister knew what was going on behind the scenes, or if she truly thought this was a devastating turn of events between the U.S. and China, not that it mattered once she was killed.

"Check out the UK files. They're the ones that are the most shocking." Gary hollered at me from amongst the mountain range of papers he created in the living room. "Then again, considering the history of colonialism, you might not be that shocked."

"Yeah, I'm still trying to wrap my head around Canada's involvement." That's when it occurred to me that we were far deeper into this than we had expected to ever be. "This is why they killed Iza isn't it? Because they thought she knew what these papers were." I looked over to him from my spot hunched over the kitchen table, his head was dropped and his face was stiff, almost stern.

"Don't, Dani; you don't get to do that. Just like you didn't know until you had to, Iza was completely in the dark on these documents. Her death isn't on me! It's on the assholes that ransacked my classroom and office, it's on the guy who pulled the trigger!" His eyes darted at me as though I was the one that shot her.

"I'm not saying it's your fault," I walked over to him like I used to with Maciek whenever he was hurt, and knelt down next to him, gently bringing his chin up so that our eyes could meet, "All I'm saying is that these documents are the real deal; they're worth killing perfectly law abiding citizens for, and I doubt that they've stopped looking for us. Listen, we've been at this for days, we should take a break. Maybe we can go into town, stop at that café? We need to get some more fuel for the generator anyways."

"Yeah. I guess with this beard I've grown no one will recognize me, and without makeup and a flatiron you look nothing like your Driver's License."

"So, I look like crap is what you're saying?" Sarcasm was one of my gifts, and it always made Gary grin.

The drive into Domaine was refreshing, it was nice to see man made buildings again, to smell fresh croissants baking in the shops, to see children running to catch up to their mothers', and hear women laughing as though nothing had changed in the world. Perhaps that is what was so attractive about small towns, because although everybody knew everybody's personal business, the happenings of the outside world didn't seem to have too much of an effect on day to day life. At least that's what it seemed like until we hit Centre Street. There were wanted posters plastered everywhere with our pictures on them, there were police officers and military personnel at every corner, and large propaganda posters hung from the eaves of every other building with slogans like "The Red Curtain is Closing Upon Us! Inform Local Law Enforcement of Possible Socialists", "Help Save Your Children from Slavery! Communism=Sweatshops for Kids." The most shocking sight was the impromptu gallows at the town hall, with men and women chained up like animals, with "Traitor" freshly tattooed on their foreheads.

Gary and I looked at each other, concern clearly written across both of our foreheads. "We can't turn around now, it'd be too suspicious. We just have to do what we came here for, we'll get some fresh bread from the bakery, some fuel, and a few things from the market." I glanced at Gary's knuckles, they had turned white from gripping the steering wheel; I could see he was outraged.

"We're going to expose them; we're going to put a stop to this shit! Look at them, Dani, they look like they haven't eaten for days, like they've been out there in the rain, and that woman—look at what they've done to her, they fucking have her chained up nude. You want to know what a Fascist state is? This, this shit right here! This is the shit that our country is supposed to be against." He was beginning to choke on his words, and the tears were forming in his eyes.

"Listen to me!" I made him look at me "You need to stop. We need to act as though this is nothing new, as though we've seen this in other towns. We need to remain rational." He looked away from me and down the street at the naked woman, who had obviously been beaten, perhaps even raped, and then at the Military guards standing near her laughing and pointing—one of them motioned as though he had, or had wanted to, fuck her, we could see his mouth forming the words "The Dirty Bitch"—it was at that moment that we had lost hope for ever making this right. "Gary, we need to get out of the car, and calmly, without looking at her, go into the shops." I gently pulled his gaze back towards me, and kissed him—I needed them to think that we were having a lovers' quarrel; we couldn't let them know it was the scene before us that had a hold on us.

As we walked across the street, one of the military men called over to us, and met us half way. "You there! Stop!" We finished crossing and waited for him on the sidewalk just a few yards from where the "traitors" were chained. "Yes, sir?" I decided to take charge since Gary would only say something that would cause us to be chained there.

"What's your business?" It was like something out of the movies, he would have been typecast as a brute soldier with no remorse—his dirty blonde hair, swept under his beret, chiseled facial features, and exceptional physique, his booming, deep voice, and piercing eyes; there was no doubt about it, he was definitely a teenage girls fantasy, and if his actions didn't disgust me, he would have taken over my dreams that night.

"Oh, I'm so sorry sir, we didn't realize this was a restricted area," I said in my very best French "we had heard that Domain had some of the most effective gallows, and some of the most delicious Croissants, so we thought we would take a day trip and see for ourselves." The look on his face told me that he didn't understand a word of French, but he had to save face in front of the others.

"Very well then." He motioned with his hand for us to go. "Go ahead, take a look; that dirty whore over there, she was caught teaching her class about Communism. She insisted that her lesson was all a part of the Curriculum, and that boy over there; he was caught spraying quotes from "The Communist Manifesto" on the side of the stores. They all deserve a lot worse than what they've gotten! There are certain stores which can only be accessed by Government employees, they have the Democratic Safety Effort logo on the doors; DO NOT enter those stores, you will be killed on the spot." He took a lot of enjoyment out of telling us what got these poor souls punished like this. As soon as he was done with his little speech we smiled, nodded, and kept walking.

When we were far enough away I nudged Gary in his side, we had our arms locked together, and whispered "What do you think they'd do to us if they figured out who we were?"

"I don't know, and I sure as hell don't want to find out. Let's get out of here fast."

It only took us about an hour to get everything that we needed, we stopped in at the café that we had stopped at when we were running away, and the thought donned on me that we had left a very different, very safe world behind us.

"Bonjour!" We looked up from our newspapers, and saw that we had the luck of getting the same waitress; Gary and I glanced at each other, and our eyes betrayed our hopes that she didn't recognize us. "Since you're new in town," she said with her thick Quebecois accent "speaking French is discouraged, English is the preferred language of our military support, so if you do speak English, please do for your safety and mine. What will you have?" The fear poured out of her voice.

"I'll have an espresso, and a croissant with orange marmalade, please." I glanced at her hands, which were shaking as she wrote down our order, her eyes darted from side to side, and across the street.

"And, I will have a Café au Lait and an éclair." She turned on her heels without a word and went into the café to put in our order.

"Well then" I looked over at Gary, randomly pointing at something in the paper, and holding it up to cover our lips, "What the hell is happening?"

She came out and brought us our coffee and pastries, and what at first glance looked like the bill, but she had attached a note to it.

I know who you are. It isn't safe here. Meet me 5km North on hwy 343 at 5:00; I have information that can help you. We have a mutual friend—NG.

We took our time, and enjoyed looking out onto

the fields across the road without talking, the wheat was almost ready for harvest—my father would have been amused that I could still tell these things, he would have said "Being an Alberta girl isn't so bad, now is it, at least you'll always be able to tell what time of year it is"; we paid our bill and picked up some papers, pamphlets, and community newsletters. Every one of those held information that would help us put the pieces together. It was around 4:00 when we left town; we didn't know what to do for an hour while we waited, so we sat in the car for a while, took a little walk, and found a small meadow to lie down, and watch the clouds go by. We felt like kids pointing out dragons, and bunny rabbits in the sky. After a little while we got bored of the clouds, of the prickly grass on the back of our necks, arms, and legs, and the tension that built up every time we were that close to each other but not touching. We had spent enough time trying not to touch, that when we wanted it, when we needed that touch we didn't hesitate. Between the heat from our bodies, and the hot sun beating down on our bare skin, the drying grass stuck to us, and our hair became tangled and matted. We looked like we had been working in that field all day, but our bodies finally were able to relax, even for just a few moments.

When we got back to the car, Emilie was waiting for us. She was hugging an envelope, bursting at the seams with papers, as though it was her only precious possession, resting, her feet crossed, on the front of her car. "Listen," she stepped forward "before I give you this, you have to promise me something." Gary and I quickly glanced at each other, the heat between us was far from quenched, and I knew she could feel it too. "What do you need?" Gary's voice was smooth, calm, as though he knew exactly what was going on. "There have been people going missing over the past few months, just randomly, I want you guys to take me with you. I can help you figure this out—I'm good with computers." She looked desperate, as though she knew that she would be the next one to disappear.

"Give us a minute." We walked a few yards away, just far enough so that she couldn't hear us clearly. "What do you think?" I asked "Can we trust her?"

"I don't know, but it can't hurt, she's got something that we need, and we have no other way of getting that information." I could tell Gary was weighing the pros and cons as quickly as he could. "Look, let's take her with us; we need to get her to make it look like she's just going camping for the weekend, make sure that someone knows she's leaving, tell her to give a spot that's far from where we are so that when she doesn't return, if they set out to find her, she won't be found."

"Okay." We turned around and told her what we needed her to do, and to meet us at the same spot in two hours. We decided to move the car down a bit to keep from drawing suspicion from passersby, and walked back to the meadow; when it was time to meet Emilie we approached carefully, making sure that she hadn't set us up. As soon as we were certain that the coast was clear, we pulled the car around. "So, here's what we're going to do. You are going to go to that camping spot, you're going to set up your tent, food, and all that good stuff. Tomorrow we're going to come get you, you need to trash your car, and make it look like you put up one hell of a fight with a wild animal or group of men. Okay?" Gary and I looked at her sternly, like parents giving their child a lecture.

"Got it. You'll be there, promise?" She was genuinely afraid.

"Yeah." Gary took her hand and gave it a reassuring squeeze.

When we got back to the cabin that night we didn't bother with the papers, or the news, we quickly put away our groceries, and since we were so full from our time in town, and from snacking on the fresh foods that we had purchased, we went straight to bed; we couldn't help but spend the entire night in a rhythmic bliss.

THREE'S COMPANY

"It's beautiful!" Emilie exclaimed as we drove up the dirt road towards the cabin. Her eyes reminded me of Maciek's. His were always so full of wonder, and amazement, but they were also very quizzical. He could never let something alone, he had to know, to understand the who, what, where, when, why and how of everything father and I ever spoke of. "So, if you own this cabin, why haven't they come looking for you here?"

"Well," Gary hesitated—he always suspected the worst of people, and I know he had considered that she was just phishing to find out what we knew so she could report back to the military—"This property isn't technically under my name."

"Oh, ok." I think she had realized that she was pushing him.

When we stepped out of the car, Emilie ran towards the cabin, as though she was a little girl, and her parents had just told her that this place was their home, and she could choose any room for her own.

After Emilie washed up and unpacked her clothing, she gave us the files that she had been sent. Gary and I got to work on seeing what pieces of our puzzle were missing. "If you want," I started without looking up from the papers in front of me "feel free to go for a stroll, maybe take a basket with you and pick some berries, just don't go too far; it's easy to get lost out there."

"Oh, I thought that maybe I could help you guys. I've already been through all of those papers, and have some ideas." Her childlike innocence was an endearing quality, but I knew that if she didn't begin to assert herself or stay out of our way, both Gary and I would lose patience with her quickly. I glanced at Gary and could see that he felt the same as me.

"Ok. What you got?" Gary pulled out a chair for her and gestured for her to sit and share.

"Well, I don't know what you guys have as far as files, but the blue one over there," she pointed at the far end of the table "Yeah, that one." I passed her the file. "It contains about twenty or so references to Project Alpha and Omega. This is a translated Chinese file. From the sounds of it China was in on whatever American A and O is. And the grey file there—the Beta Project" she hesitated for a minute; the excitement was getting to her—that feeling of finally being able to speak what's on your mind—and her thick Quebecois accent began fading away. "It discusses how Canada will enter into a militant state. You know the gallows you saw at town hall? Yeah, that's only the first phase; soon there'll be public executions, civilian weapons will be confiscated, and those who are unwilling to cooperate are to be shot without hesitation. It's as though our governments, across the globe, are adopting these Totalitarian laws in the guise of national security."

"Wait a minute." Gary had noticed her change

"What the fuck is going on?!? What the hell happened to your accent?" He was visibly outraged.

"I told you, we have a mutual friend. The accent was a farce, and my placement in Domaine was an educated guess, there were many more like me placed in other small towns. My name is Emilie. I am a waitress. You don't need to know anymore about me than that. I'm here to help you find the answers that you need for now; once you have those I'll be gone. I'm going to need to see the rest of your files, and your computer; you do have one here right?" Her entire demeanor had changed; she no longer had the eyes of a scared little girl, but the fire of a determined soul, a woman who wanted to keep her world for collapsing in on itself, burned deep in her eyes. The change was frightening. Gary and I stared at one another for what seemed like ages.

"Fine." I stood up, and grabbed the files that we had managed to lump together and brought them to her. "These are the ones we've managed to connect so far, but we've lost our momentum; we're sort of stuck at this point."

"Hmm." She bit her bottom lip, furrowed her brow and looked up at us "I honestly thought you'd be a lot further along than this. It's a bit disappointing. Could you put on some coffee please?"

"Ummm, sure." Gary got up, and put on a pot; his coffee was always much stronger than when I made it, so whenever we had the impression that we would be up all night, he was the one to make the coffee, and I'd get the snacks together.

"Hungry?" I asked.

"Starved." She paused for a moment "No baked goods please, I've been living on bread and pastries for the past year. Oh, when you get a moment could you please bring the computer?" For someone so manipulative, she sure was polite—I suppose that's one of the benefits of being Canadian, even when someone deceives you they're as nice about it as they can be.

"Sure." I was still trying to wrap my head around what we saw in town, and it was beginning to be too much.

From where I stood in the kitchen, washing and chopping vegetables for a salad, and putting out beef jerky, I could see her studying the files, and making notes, the whole time chewing on her lip. Gary came up behind me, placed his arms around and began whispering in my ear. "I don't know if we can trust her." I nodded slightly "But, I don't think we have much of a choice. We'll have to keep a close eye on her, just to be certain." Of course I agreed with him, but what could we do, it's not like there are a lot of places to hide things in an old wood cabin.

"Look," She started "I'm sorry for deceiving you guys, but the identity I've adopted was more to deceive the townspeople, to convince them that I really did belong there." She left it at that, and so did we, although we never were able to fully trust her.

We spent most of the night looking through the European files, and answering questions as Emilie had them. By the end of a week we had figured out that the major world powerhouse governments were involved. Smaller, less influential governments like Poland, West Africa, etc. would eventually play supporting roles as part of their foreign policy, but they were blind to the major workings of the operation. After ten days, we were exhausted and decided to take a rest day. Emilie had yet to see the creek, or leave the cabin except to hang her laundry. She loved the idea of going on a hike, refreshing our minds, and giving our bodies the much needed change of scenery. Our bodies ached from being hunched over, seated on chairs, the floor, the couch, even on our beds; our backs felt as though we had been pulling heavy weights, not sitting.

The walk to the creek was refreshing, the air was crisp, and the sweet smell of decaying leaves was beginning to take over, the creek was cold—almost too cold for a swim—but our bodies couldn't resist diving in. The feeling of cold water rushing over my body, washing away the fatigue, healing my aching back, and rinsing over my face to the ends of my hair, gave me renewed vigor. Emilie wanted to pick berries, and Gary and I wanted to go for a hike, so we left her there on the shore with three buckets to fill. We didn't have to go too far before Gary grabbed me and pulled me into him, quickly untying my bikini top; we hadn't had a chance to kiss let alone have sex since Emilie arrived, and our bodies craved each other. I slipped my bikini bottom to the side, and pushed down his trunks; Gary pinned me against a tree, the rough bark against my back scratched, and I could feel the blood begin trickling down, but all I cared about, all I wanted was Gary. We didn't need long either, and my teeth sank into Gary's shoulder to suppress my screams. The warmth of his breath battled against the cold in the air, and the sensation was unbearably pleasurable. After we had made love against the tree for the third time we left our bathing suits behind, and walked to find a soft bed of grass in a clearing somewhere. We must have spent hours in the meadow, because by the time we were satiated the sun had begun setting. We walked back to our tree, put on our bathing suits, slowly, stopping here and there to steal a kiss, back to the creek.

Emilie must have filled the buckets and went back to the cabin, because when we got to the creek she was gone, the picnic basket, and buckets were gone, only our clothes remained. We decided to stay and take another swim before heading back to the stress, and dankness of the cabin, to the judging eyes that we knew would be waiting for us, and we made love again. It was dark by the time we got back, and Emilie was hard at work studying the documents we had been looking at for the past ten days.

"I thought maybe you'd been eaten by some wild creature." She said glibly as we walked through the door.

"Sorry to worry you." The words escaped my mouth as though I were explaining myself to my father.

"Feeling better? 'Cause you sure as hell look like shit." Her matter-of-factness was shocking; she'd been so kind and polite up until that moment.

"To be honest, no." I snapped "I'd feel better if I didn't have to live with the knowledge that our whole world is about to go to shit! That every major government is plotting together to destroy the world that we know and love. How fucking good do you feel about that?" I was yelling, my heart beating hard against my chest, my fists clenched, nails digging into the palms of my hands. Gary put his hands of my shoulders, and I began to cry. He helped me wash up, brush out my hair, and put me to bed.

"Shhhhh" he was so calm "It's going to be okay.

We're going to stop this. I promise." It was a promise that he'd never be able to keep, but he would try.

Morning came in bright, powerful, and full of the tension of a guitar string ready to burst. Emilie and Gary had been up all night pouring over the same documents, but this time there were new files sitting on the kitchen table; they were manuscripts, filled with my father's handwriting—his notes, thoughts, and concerns. These were new to me, I'd never seen my father work on these. "Where did you find these?" I furrowed my brow, drew in a deep breath, preparing for some great mystery to unravel before my eyes. "Good morning." Emilie's only response to me.

"I asked you a question!" My voice rose, deep like my father's used to become when he demanded an answer. I grabbed the manuscripts—treasures that belonged to me—stepped towards her, my free hand clenched into a tight fist. "Answer me!!!"

"The same place I got all of these, and that's all that you need to know." She was so calm, almost demure about it. "Your breakfast is keeping warm in the oven. Hope you like Eggs Benedict." Gary poured the coffee, and I ate in silence. After my breakfast was finished I washed in the basin outside—we had to be careful with how much of the plumbing we used, the septic tank could only take so much use. As I wrung out my hair I heard the gentle snapping of a twig just a few feet away, my heart jumped into my throat, and my mind imagined an armed guard pointing the end of his AK-47 at my temple, but there stood in all of its majestic glory, a white-tailed deer. "Hm," I thought, "it's been a long time since anyone's seen one of your kind. I wonder where you came fr—" the noise from inside the house pulled me out of my musings, the deer flicked her tail up in the air and ran off—silent as a mouse. I quickly pulled my white tank on; it clung to my still wet body, and struggled with my pants as I tried to peer inside through the small window which allowed a limited view of the cabin's living room. From a distance, the cabin was almost ethereal. There was this pastoral quality to it—unlike many of the cabins that are found on resorts—almost as if some poor, tired settler and his family built it from logs that they themselves cut down. It was perfect. Inside, I could see Gary and Emilie working quickly to clean up all of the papers. I ran in "What is going on?!?" I looked around bewildered, seeing piles of paper being thrown together into boxes.

"Never mind. Just help us get all of this packed up!" Gary demanded my compliance with a simple look; just like my mother's. It didn't take us very long to get the papers all boxed and put into the car. Within a half hour we had gathered our things and were driving off.

"So, does anyone care to explain to me what is going on?" I looked back at Emilie who was busy chewing on her nails and cuticles—her worries were beginning to manifest physically.

"We received a warning from another group that some cells have been compromised. We have to change locations." Her eyes darted back and forth, and she was wringing her hands in a nervous compulsion.

We drove Westward the rest of the day, ensuring to stay off of any major highways. We sent Emilie into stores and gas stations since our pictures were still plastered all throughout the country. As far as the government—what little was left of it—was concerned, we were public enemy number one.

After hours of silence, I finally decided I needed to know—I had the right to know—where those manuscripts came from. "Gary," the gentleness in my voice betrayed me "I need to know where she got those manuscripts. I never saw my dad work on those, but that's his writing in the margins. It's unmistakable." The way he looked at me told me that he knew as much as I did, and that asking Emilie was likely to cause me a lot of grief. We sat in silence until she came back with a bag full of groceries.

"All right," she sighed, "We've got apples, carrots, some sandwiches, water, milk, some cereal, oh, and I got some plastic bowls and spoons." She looked at us, took in a deep breath, and passed us our lunch. "Here let's eat and then I'll answer some of your questions." We took our time eating, Gary and I switched seats so that he could rest a little while I drove. I let him ask questions; most of them were about his own involvement, and we found out that it was his interest in corrupt government systems, and his Doctoral thesis on the revolutionary state that made Emilie's associates trust his determination, and gall—

they knew he would stay on task, because they knew he needed to find the answer. I had always known he had a revolutionary spirit—he's a Frenchman after all, and his passion is what excited me most about him when we first met.

Gary hummed and hawed at every one of her answers, wondering how much truth was in each one, and how much of it she had made up on the spot to make herself seem more important than she really was to her employers. At the end of the diatribe, Gary was satisfied as to his role in this whole mess. They turned their attention to me, and all I wanted to know was why my father's marginal notes were important—something none of us would know until it was too late. We checked into a roadside motel that smelled of mothballs, bleach, and sex; it was far from ideal, but we were too exhausted from the day's excitement to keep driving.

EMERGING CHANGE

When we finally reached Toronto, we knew that Canada could never be the same. When I was a little girl I thought that Canada was the safest place to live, but as we drove towards that great Metropolis—the symbol of Canada's diversity and prosperity, our cultural centre—I realized that my whole concept of what Canada stood for was fundamentally flawed. The blood red billboards with propaganda—slogans calling for the immediate execution of anyone breaking the most arbitrary of laws, catch phrases praising the rise of an elite class of warriors— complimented the hanging bodies, and stench from their flesh melting in the mid-September sun. It hit us like a sledgehammer. We had heard reports of traitors being tried and judged on the streets, but this was beyond our wildest imaginings. It was like something out of a movie. Our time spent in Gary's cabin had kept our minds clean of these images; images that still plague my dreams. We knew that we needed to stay secluded, where we would be unnoticed. Emilie knew exactly where to take us.

We pulled up in front of an old storefront just off of the main shopping district; the building was run down, the windows cracked, the red paint on the door was peeling, the mortar was crumbling, and the sign looked like it was ready to come crashing down. "Come on." Emilie looked over her shoulder as she climbed out of the driver's seat "Everyone's waiting for us." Gary and I were surprised that there were others like us here. The street was almost devoid of cars, and the air was still with rot, urine, and fried food. We exchanged a hesitant glance and followed Emilie inside. The hinges on the door squeaked as an old bell rang to announce our arrival. There were half dressed mannequins fallen to the ground, racks and shelves were ransacked with only a few odd items left behind--a purse here, a single shoe there—the room was dimly lit, the windows only let a small portion of dim alley light in through the cracks. The irony of it struck us and we couldn't contain our nervous laughter.

"Oh, hello there!" A small voice popped up from behind the sales counter, and both Gary and I jumped. The small, frail woman came up to us, bent over in laughter. "You two sure take things seriously, don't you." She stood up, her silver hair pulled back into a neatly combed bun, she wore a pair of tan slacks which hung on her thin frame, and a sequined pink and black plaid cat sweater to keep her warm—the days were getting colder, and I doubted she could handle any temperature below 5 degrees. "I'm Lucille. Now, come quickly. We've been waiting for you two." As we followed her up into the apartment above the store, we could hear what sounded like a throng of voices, all talking above one another. The hallway leading to the apartment door was just as run down as the storefront; the names of lovers were scratched into the walls, and the stench of marijuana was stuck in the drywall and in the shag carpeting, the stucco ceiling was peeling, and water stains dominated over the white ceiling color. When we got to the door, Lucille turned to us "Now, it isn't much, but this is where you'll stay until we can resolve some things. The bedding is clean, there are dishes in the kitchen, and a small television in the living room." She handed us a key "Not that you'll be going out much considering that your faces are plastered all over the country, but you never know when you might need it." We looked at her puzzled; her bright sweater had both of us just as confused as the question that boggled our minds. "Hurry along you two. We haven't all day!" She opened the door and the hallway became flooded with sound. There were twenty others sitting in the living room, all of them poring over their own files, cross-referencing to someone else's files, working together like on family puzzle night. Gary's eyes lit up, and a smile crept across his face. "Pass me the files!" His hand shot out towards me with expectation. "I don't have them; Emilie grabbed them." He could tell I was confused and amused by his reaction.

"Sorry." His apology was half-hearted as he walked off towards Emilie who was already seated with the others comparing notes and annotations.

"I knew your father." Lucille had a way of

sneaking up on someone when they were lost in thought. "He was very good at what he did. I'm sorry that I couldn't make it to say goodbye, but the nature of our work here required me to stay away." I was confused, and my facial expression betrayed it. "Oh, don't feel bad deary! My children are grown, with families of their own, and they have no clue what I do. It was important for him to keep this from you; I would always reproach him for trying to get you involved." She had pulled on her glasses to help sort through papers, and the rhinestones at the tips caught just enough of the light to project a small rainbow, causing Lucille to glow, even in her old age.

"Is this why she had his work?" My voice became small, just as it had been when I was eight years old and my mother caught me taking five dollars from my father's nightstand to buy myself an ice cream cone at the creamery.

"You mean she didn't tell you?" Lucille shook her head "Emi has always been rather insensitive; she may be pretty, but her intellect runs her life. I've always told her that she needs to let go of reason from time to time. Hmf." She took my arm and pulled me in towards the kitchen. "Here, deary. Have a cup of tea and a snack. We'll need you to decipher some of your father's shorthand, his notes are what will help pull all of this together." I took the hot cup into my hands, closed my eyes, and imagined all of the chaos slipping away. When I opened my eyes, the reality hit me like it had that night at Gary's apartment. Tears began to fill my eyes, and I wept for my father. Lucille's gentle hand rubbed my back, and she watched me weep.

When I finally had the strength to begin suturing my wounds, I picked up my father's work, and worked through the night to decipher his notes. I ended up having a thirty page diatribe of seemingly random phrases, most of which lead me down a path of memories. As I began pulling these out, the sequences started to line up, and in a flurry of thought and inspiration I gathered up Gary's research—ripping it from his grasp while he argued pure semantics with some poor Graduate student from the University of Victoria—leaving him bewildered, hushing his attempts to reprimand. The crowd began to gather around the kitchen table where I sat working. Lucille stood in the kitchen stirring a large pot of beef stew, the smell of which beckoned me to work harder and faster as my hunger pains tugged at me to stop. She smiled as she recalled how my father would sit at that very table and write the frantic notes that I sat deciphering. "Pass me everything on China." I demanded, my hand outstretched, waiting for the weight of the paper. A young, blonde haired, hazel eyed young man, no more than twenty-two, his body covered in piercings and tattoos, approached me cautiously—my father would have shook his head at his appearance, dismissing it as a sign of lacking integrity. "I won't bite, promise." I glanced up at him and smiled menacingly. He dropped the files on the table with a thud. The folders were thick, and I knew that I would need help to get through all of them. I had to expose to these strangers my most intimate memories.

It wasn't until I had finished explaining my father's notations, and how they would work to tie all of the files together that Lucille called us to dinner. The stew was hot, and satisfying, it held within it the comforting warmth of a cup of hot chocolate being sipped upon by a fire, yet it was hearty and satisfying like a bowl of thick porridge on a cold Alberta winter's morning right before you step out into the bitter cold for a game of shinny. Lucille passed around large baguettes which she'd split and buttered, and we tore off pieces and passed the baguettes around in a ceremonious fashion. There was no large table for us all to sit at, so we turned down the couch cushions, laid out some blankets, and sat around the apartment. The scent of the stew and baguettes filled our lungs, permeated the blankets so that Gary and I would go to bed for a week with that soothing smell enveloping us, and even the stench of the hallway was overtaken by the pleasantness of our dinner. When everyone had finished, and the dishes had been washed, everyone took to their folders without prompt, working with a hive mentality. The silence that overtook the apartment was full with tension and suspense, and was only occasionally broken by the sound of turning pages, dry coughs, and sneezes sometimes followed by a short bought of laughter. When he'd finished combing through the pages from France, Gary came to me as I poured over documents from the U.S.; the smell of his cologne was mixing with the smell of his sweat, and his breath was sweet and warm as it hit the side of my neck. Had we been alone I would have melted into his arms. "I think I've figured out the connection between the Americas and France, and I'm going to guess that the others will find something similar." He had his glasses on—they were square, and gave him an air of superiority—and they began to slip down his nose as he looked down over my shoulder. "Well," I pushed his glasses back up "are you going to tell me, or do I need to ask leading questions?"

"Look for references to September 11, 2030. " He began pointing at several operations that all suggest a sudden, unexpected end date—a projection of when economies would be too stressed, and populations would begin to drop. "Look here. There are at least ten references to that date, and all of them point towards a sudden stop. There aren't any more ops listed that go beyond that date, it's almost as though France stops existing." We began to frantically leaf through the documents on the U.S.A. and found reference after reference to September 11, 2030, and a sudden stop in all government activities. We asked our colleagues to begin looking for that specific date, and after only a short while they were all coming to us with that same conclusion. We finally understood what was about to happen, and that we had to stop it from happening.

We spent weeks cooped up in that one bedroom apartment, with that rag tag bunch of men and women—some were old, like Lucille, and would be asked to keep their ear to the ground, others were too young to take bold, calculated risks, and would stay behind and make the information we'd uncovered public, and then there were those of us like Gary and me, neither fighters, nor hackers (we were only ever good with a pen and paper), we were the ones who would bring bits and pieces to independent media groups. We were counting on the little publications, the ones that people read over their latte and scone before heading into the office, to warn the public. That's how this all began.

UNREST

We had never meant for it to go as far as it did; we never even considered that people all around the world would turn so quickly on their governments. It had been three weeks since we'd first arrived in Toronto, and we were ready to embark on our next adventure. Lucille had packed us some food, she had taken the time to mend some of our clothes—we were public enemy number one, after all—and as we were heading out of the store front towards our car she handed me a package of saltines. "You've been complaining about your stomach lately, so I thought these might help." She looked at me suspiciously, as though she knew something that I didn't. "Thanks." It was my only reply, the only one that I could muster after everything she had done for us, for me. She was a kind woman, and I knew that I would never have the chance to thank her again. As we drove away, we could see her standing with her arms crossed, holding down her brown knit shawl, and her breath visible on that chilled October morning. We were Alberta bound, but would stop along the way in small towns and in big cities. We were always more careful in small towns; there is truth in what people say about townies being nosey.

We managed to get half way to Sudbury before I had to get Gary to pull over; for the first time in my life I was road sick—it wouldn't be long before I figured out why. "Pull over! Pull over NOW!!!" I screamed. Just as Gary pulled the car to a stop, I pulled the door open, and vomited the scrambled eggs, toast, and coffee that Lucille had made for our farewell breakfast—a hearty change from the oatmeal and plain yogurt with frozen berries that we had been having daily. As I sat back in the seat I could feel the concerned stares coming from Gary and Emilie. "I'm fine. Just keep driving." I looked at Gary, took a swig of water from my steel bottle, and spat the remnants of vomit out the window. Gary drove a conservative 110 kilometers per hour the whole time; it was mid-October, and we knew that the RCMP would be looking to make their monthly quota for tickets. We had to work fast, there was less than a year left before our deadline, but first we needed to stop the first attack, or at least prepare the public for it. I knew my role would eventually be to expose the big bad, to be the person standing on a hill screaming with few people listening; but I knew that I would try, and perhaps with a small amount of persistence I would succeed.

"I'm getting hungry," I looked over at Gary as we passed the sign that told us Sudbury was only 18 kilometers away, "Let's stop in Sudbury for a quick bite." I was matter-of-fact, almost having forgotten having thrown up. Gary looked at me puzzled. "Seriously?" His tone was derisive "You just puked! What the fuck, Dani?!?" He looked back at Emilie. "I could go for a Big Mac and fries." She shrugged, and it reminded me of when my mother didn't want to reveal what she was thinking. But Emilie was never one to mince words. "Hey, when's the last time you bought tampons? Seriously, I don't think I've seen you PMS yet."

"What kind of fucking question is that, Em? Are you fucking kidding me? That's none of your business!" I was blushing, I could feel the blood rushing to my face, but I knew she had a point. I hadn't had my period in two months, and I knew for some time that there was something off about how I was feeling.

"Hey, if you got yourself knocked up, then that could throw a huge wrench in our plans. I'm pretty certain everyone would need to know about it so, you know, we could make adjustments." She was snide, and I knew that she had a very good point. What if I was pregnant? What would I do? My mind spun with questions, fears, and I felt nauseous again.

"Pull over!" I yelled as loudly as I could, but it was too late, Gary couldn't get into the shoulder fast enough. That's when I knew, there was no way around it. I had always wanted children, especially after having spent time with Gary, and there was nothing that would cause me to give up a baby that we had made. I looked over at him, his eyes were filled with worry, and I could tell his mind was asking the same questions that my heart had already answered.

The at-home test confirmed our suspicions. When I stepped out of the gas station bathroom, Gary was standing tersely by the slushy machines. His eyes were searching for an answer in my face, I smiled, and gently placed my hands over my stomach; his chest fell in a sigh, and a small smile crept across his face. He pulled me into his arms and whispered "I'll never let you go."

"Well, fuck!" Emilie was waiting impatiently by the till "Would you two just hurry the fuck up! We've got a deadline. Oh, and congrats I guess." She never liked the idea of children being around her; they made her uncomfortable. We paid for the slushies and vitamins, and left Sudbury behind. Our goal was Winnipeg.

We took turns driving through the remaining hours of the day, and into the night. There was an unspoken understanding between us that things would have to speed up, and that we would have to find a doctor somewhere to make sure that everything was alright, and to tell us exactly how far along I was. We could see the Winnipeg skyline by noon the next day. The sun was high and bright even though it was a cold day; the exhaust was visible from the rear view mirror, and there was frost on the cars of commuters heading into town from their quiet, suburban homes. I watched the mothers looking back at their children, some of them were singing, others were yelling at the kids to stop fighting—something that I had always found ironic with the neighbour lady; she always yelled at her kids for fighting with one another.

"...that's about all there is to it. Sound good?" Emilie had been talking to me for the last ten minutes, and I hadn't heard a word she said. "What? Sorry I spaced out."

"Seriously?" she dropped her head in frustration. "Here's the gist of it: We've got the abridged research packets in the trunk already to go with postage paid. We're gonna stay together, that way no one gets lost—thanks for that lovely detour by the way—" She nodded at me " and drop them into various mailboxes throughout the city. There are five small publications here, so we will stay here until we see that they have run the story. Got it?"

"Yeah, but why not take it to a big paper, or a news station? It'd reach a greater audience wouldn't it?" It was common enough to hear 'go big, or go home' growing up in Alberta.

"The big papers wouldn't touch this, and if they did, the government would be all over it. The laws about freedom of the press have changed since Beijing. The press is forced to reveal their sources, and if it's submitted anonymously, then you can guarantee that the pages and envelope will be scanned for identification markers." Emilie had studied forensics when she was sixteen, and was enrolled at Harvard law during the Beijing attacks; she dropped out after the first year when she came to the realization that the world was going to hell, and her knowledge was better used to protect the public, than to represent murderers and rapists.

By the time we had finished it was time to have some dinner, and head to the safe house. As we pulled up, we could see the sun setting, and we just sat in the car, looking out of our windows mesmerized by the oranges and purples that were cast upon the clouds. There had been radiation clouds detected as far West as Regina, so we weren't surprised to see houses boarded up, and windows and doors covered in military grade plastics, designed specifically for radiation. There were houses marked with red, yellow, green and black "X"s on the front doors. Red was meant to indicate that someone in that house had died of radiation poisoning, yellow indicated a small level of toxicity had been detected in certain items in the house, green meant that the house was clean, but these changed daily, and black was for quarantine and cryogenic demolition. Our safe house was designated green, but we knew we wouldn't be able to stay there long, there were daily radiation sweeps performed by military personnel. There were thousands of houses marked red and black across the Eastern provinces, and we knew that this sudden upheaval of people's lives, that the radiation sicknesses, the disfigurements that babies would suffer for the next several decades, were all planned. They were all "residual effects, which would create ideal conditions for the dissolution of individual government systems." It all sounded so theoretical, something out of a peer reviewed journal—a hypothesis. The reality of it was horrific. As we stepped out of the car, the putrid air hit us, and we knew that the houses marked red and black held the rotting bodies of entire families, quarantined for the protection of the masses. These families would have been given placebos to ease their minds, and been told that there was nothing more that modern science could offer them. Once the doctors proclaimed the house to be "infested", the family had no chance of survival. They would be given a small supply of military rations and water, enough to last up to two weeks, babies would be examined thoroughly, and if they weren't showing symptoms, or severe deformities, would be removed immediately and taken to the hospital—mothers were left to watch their older children suffer, and eventually die.

The safe house was clean, there was running water and electricity, not that it would matter much, we were there to sleep during the night. When we got ourselves settled we stretched out and turned on the evening news. We ate sandwiches that we'd picked up at the store earlier that day, and allowed ourselves to be pulled into the programming. The images were horrific, children whose bodies were burned, their parents unable to help them because they too were severely disfigured. Bombs dropped on so-called military operational centers, ended up being schools with teachers and children who had just sat down to their lessons. These attacks were considered successful, because "the schools in Baghdad indoctrinate children to hate America, and to take up the call to Jihad" reported one news station. Another reported that "although the loss of children is always tragic, this attack has been deemed successful by the Canadian Military, and Air force, because it will act as a strong message to those groups which are considering a counter attack. Canada will not stand by as our neighbours and allies are under attack!" We couldn't watch any more.

    While we were cooped up in Toronto, there was little time for television, although we would watch the occasional broadcast that would give us motivation to work harder and faster. Now all we could do was wait until the papers ran the story, and until our friends who stayed behind in Toronto were able to hack into the databases of major publications, news broadcasters, and into the servers of social media sites to run our first broadcast: me sitting in a brightly lit room with white walls, exposing the lies, warning people to take up arms, to make their voices heard. We paid tribute to Anonymous alongside the Occupy movement, groups which emerged at the turn of the century, and grew strong as Wall Street caved under the pressures of the War on Terror. Many in our company had been associated with them in the past, until they incorporated and named a CEO. The need for material wealth is a disease that spreads easily.

    We rose early to find the sun just peaking above the horizon, we knew the radiation sweeps began shortly after sunrise, so we changed our clothes and left. We spent the day moving from coffee house to coffee house, and during a period of relative quiet we stepped into a walk-in clinic. The doctor checked me over, determining that everything looked fine. I was fifteen weeks pregnant. My first trimester had passed without my knowing, and I would soon have to buy maternity clothes, and everything I would need to take care of a baby. We had planned to stay in Winnipeg for a week, never staying in the same neighbourhood for more than a day or two. On our way out of the doctor's office we picked up copies of all of the different newspapers that we could find. As we walked towards the car we saw a maternity shop next to a sandwich shop. It was just after the lunch rush, so the street was almost empty of foot traffic. While Gary and I went into the store to pick up some new clothes, Emilie sat out on a bench leafing through the newspapers for any sign of our research being exposed.

"It's you!" the salesgirl whispered as she approached us. "You're the woman from the video on YouTube." There was excitement in her eyes, and we couldn't tell if she was ready to call us in, or if she was going to help us out.

"You must have me mistaken for someone else." I backed away from her, ready to run at a moment's notice.

"Oh, geeze. Relax. I always thought there was

something weird going on ever since Beijing, I just didn't know what. I kept telling my family that they were crazy for being so accepting of all the wars. I mean, Canada's never had this many soldiers coming home in pine boxes. I'm so with you!" She was genuine in her enthusiasm; I would never have imagined her to be the kind of girl who would believe and take action. "Good." Gary piped up. "Look, we just found out that we're expecting a baby, and we're desperate for some clothes, diapers, and all that good stuff. Can you help us out?" It wasn't like Gary to ask for help, but we were in no position to be proud. "Oh, for sure! You guys can help yourselves to whatever you need. I'll just tell my boss that we got robbed again. She hasn't reported a robbery in months!" We offered a small amount of money to compensate her for her trouble, but she refused. "You guys are exposing the greatest conspiracy since, like, ever! As far as I'm concerned the world owes you." Emilie pulled the car around, and we loaded the cloth diapers, baby clothes, maternity clothes, car seat, and pack 'n' play in the car; it took a lot of shuffling, but somehow we managed to fit everything that we needed, and everything that we already had.

"Anything in the papers?" Gary looked back at Emilie.

"Not yet. Hopefully tomorrow." Disappointment rang in her voice, and had settled in her eyes.

"Well," I cleared my throat "The girl inside recognized me from the broadcast. Apparently it's on YouTube. I guess our friends have had some success. Now, I think, is a good time to change our appearances." The news perked her up. When we returned to the safe house the sun was already setting, and the door was still marked green. We spent the night cutting and dyeing our hair, Gary had allowed his beard to grow in, and his hair to grow out. At this point he looked like a shaggy dog. We turned on the news, and watched government paid reporters discuss the falsehood of our broadcast, encouraging citizens to remain calm, that the attacks against "the enemy" were truly for the protection of the true democratic system we have in North America. Their eyes betrayed their lies; we knew that the broadcasts were all scripted.

"Bull—fucking—shit!" Emilie yelled at the

television.

"Yelling at the TV. isn't going to do you any good, Em." Gary sighed "Look, we should turn this shit off, and get to bed." There were no beds that we would use, just blankets that we piled one on top of another, our bodies were getting accustomed to this kind of discomfort. We set our alarm to go off at 5:30 in the morning, knowing full well that that would give us just enough time to watch a bit of the morning news, have a quick breakfast, and get out the door before sunrise. We were all wondering if today would be the day that we saw some indication that one of the free publications would be brave enough to run with our story. We were running out of time, and we knew that if we were going to be successful, we had to reach older audiences soon.

We had spent that day much like the previous, moving around from shop to shop, never staying longer than was necessary, and spending as little as possible. Gary gathered up a copy of every paper, and we spent hours parked in the car at a shopping plaza, reading. There was a bitter chill in the air, and our hands became stiff and sore from the cold, but we kept searching. "Here!" Emilie shoved the paper between me and Gary "Page D6. It's small, but it's there." An air of relief swept over us, and for the first time in months we breathed easily, and smiled freely. Over the past year I had noticed lines forming around Gary's brow, he was beginning to adopt a constant look of worry, and as his face relaxed, and he took in a deep breath of reprieve the lines relaxed and reminded me of the bright eyed, breathless man standing behind a lectern, voice raised to reach the back of the theatre of 450 students.

That night, with my hair dyed navy blue, and newly cut—Emilie had many hidden talents, and one of them was hairdressing—into a pixie cut, making me almost indistinguishable from the girl with long, blonde, loose curls framing her face that was announcing global revolution on the internet, we went out to dinner. The televisions in the pub were all turned to the news channels—no one wanted to watch hockey anymore, they were all too caught up in what could happen next. Gary loved good Irish food and ordered himself the Yorkshire pudding and beef stew, Emilie was a vegetarian so her options were limited to a Veggie burger and salad, and I had a steak sandwich. We took our time enjoying every hot bite, warming our bodies, as the snow began to fall a grayish-brown from the sky. I hadn't seen white snow since I was a girl in Alberta; as much as the Province called the Oil Sands safe, and clean, the air quality dropped steadily as they dug deeper and deeper into the earth, and worked the machines harder and longer each day. I was only ten years old when I saw the first gray snowfall. I was outside playing with my friend Jen, who died of lung cancer when we were twelve, and I remember running into the house screaming for my father to come and see the snow. My father wouldn't let me and Maciek play outside in the snow or rain after that; Jen played outside regardless of the weather, and the doctor's blamed her exposure to toxins that bound to the snow and rain. Gary and Emilie order a bottle of Guinness each, an expense that I thought was foolish and unnecessary at twenty dollars a bottle, and I had tea, cheap at only five dollars a cup. It was getting late, and we were ready to leave.

Just as we were about to get up, the screen went bright white, and there I was; my face, my voice, our message to be diligent, to be loud, to overthrow wherever necessary overtook the screens. There was a brief moment of tension, a moment when we were certain there would be helicopters and tanks surrounding us, but nothing happened. The screen went black, and the news broadcast resumed with anchors trying hectically to regain their composure, to dispel the truth as lies. That's when the gunshots came. One of the production members was shot down by military personnel for not being able to stop our team of expert hackers—kids who spent the hours after school learning how to maneuver around the most difficult firewalls—from sharing the truth. That was the turning point. I knew that that would be the last straw. A live assassination of an innocent citizen by a government employee; we couldn't ask for a better hand up from the very organization we were trying to destroy.

Over the course of the night we watched reports of riots beginning to break out in Manhattan, Warsaw, Berlin, Paris, and Baghdad—these were the cities that had been worst hit by attacks, the cities where children had been slaughtered. Smaller towns would take more convincing. Cities are full of skeptics. The pub was beginning to empty out, and the bartender came to us with a manila envelope which he slid towards me. "We have mutual friends. You're welcome to stay until you're ready to move on." He threw a dishtowel over his shoulder and walked away. We were thankful to have an ally in a city where we were constantly on the move. There would be no sleep for us that night; our eyes were glued to the screen. The envelope contained keys to a bigger car, and a letter from Lucille.

I knew when you left that you would soon be in need of a bigger, and better, vehicle to get you on your way. I knew you would stop in here, it was on the safe list I handed Gary, and he told me how much he loves Irish food. We've made good progress here, the kids are all hard at work, and we're hoping to crack through any day. The other teams are reporting back with success on the East Coast, and in the Northern States. Lots of small papers are running the story, and people are murmuring. We need to start seeing more success here. We only have six months to reach our deadline. There are rumors floating around the web of organizing marches on Parliament Hill, but marching won't do any good. We need something big to happen to get people mad, to get them to arms. If you need anything else send word through Troy—the burly bartender. You'll know when it's time for you to move onwards, until then stay with Troy and he'll take care of you.

Lucille

We took the keys, and entered into the dark night, to search for our new vehicle, and transfer all of our things. It was a grey solar minivan, with all power options, satellite television, car phone, and internet for Emilie to continue doing her work. We would be able to sleep more comfortably in the back of the van than we had since we left the cabin. When we walked back into the dim light of the pub Troy stood at the bar with snacks, tea and warm milk laid out. "I'll need the keys to your car." His voice was deep, and would have been perfectly suited for sports announcing. It was smooth and comforting, and there was a sing-song quality to his intonation. His musculature struck me under the low-hanging bar lights, he was well-defined and broad, his chin was strong, he had high cheekbones, and his dark skin had a golden glow. He was beautiful. Gary handed the keys over to him reluctantly. "What are you going to do?" Troy turned to put on his jacket and scarf "I'm going to take care of you just as Aunty asked." We had a tough time imagining any familial relationship between that frail Creole woman, and this godlike specimen of a man. I could tell from her expression that Emilie had only one thought coursing through her body. "Go with him." I whispered to her. She jumped off of her stool, grabbed her jacked and ran after him.

For the first time in three months Gary and I were alone. As soon as the door slammed behind Emilie we locked the door and took advantage of the space we had to ourselves. We were ravenous, our bodies ached, and it didn't take long for either one of us to finish, but we kept going until we heard a rapping at the door. We threw our clothes on quickly, straightened our hair, and unlocked the door. Emilie's hair was disheveled, and there was a glow about her, a satisfaction that explained why they had taken as long as they did. They had driven the car only fifteen minutes away from the bar to an abandoned warehouse, but they had been gone for three hours. Troy was unabashed about why they'd taken so long, and we were glad that they had. He led us down a dim hallway that led to a couple of offices, each with a hide-a-bed. He stayed the night with Emilie. I woke to the smell of eggs, bacon, toast, and freshly brewed coffee, and the sound of laughter coming from the kitchen; I rolled over to hold onto Gary, and found that his side of the bed was empty and cold.

It was much brighter in the day, and I could make out the markings of lovers past in the walls, and the pale green paint that framed the bar. The sunlight poked in through the skylights as it melted the snow. Troy had managed to get out and grab the newspapers; he was listening to the radio while preparing breakfast. "Morning," I clambered into the kitchen "Smells good."

"Thanks," Troy tossed a piece of hot toast behind him at Gary "Sit down; your bennies are almost done." Gary must have told him that it was my favourite breakfast aside from fresh, soft, buttery croissants with homemade jam and espresso. Gary had already finished his eggs and bacon, and was cracking into a ripe Orange; the mist from the peel filled the space around him and made my mouth water. It had been years since Oranges were available to the public. Emilie stumbled in, hung over and wanting nothing but a Bloody Mary and Aspirin. Troy slid her a tall glass of cold water, and two Advil, normally she would have argued that it wasn't what she had wanted, but she couldn't find the energy so she drank the water and took the pills. He turned slowly with my breakfast, expertly arranged on the plate with chunky fried potatoes, an English muffin topped with Canadian back bacon, tomato, caramelized onions, perfectly poached eggs that spilled their golden yolks as soon as the knife pushed through the whites, and a sinfully creamy hollandaise. I hadn't realized just how sore my body had been for the past month and a half sleeping in the car and on piled blankets and hard floors, but that night spent on the hide-a-bed was like sleeping on a memory foam mattress in comparison. Gary gave Emilie two hard boiled eggs and two pieces of white toast with jam, to help settle her stomach. They had spent most of the night drinking, talking, and toying with each other. After breakfast we left the bar, and followed Troy to his house. His neighbourhood hadn't experienced any cases of radiation poison, so his house was swept on a weekly basis, we would be safe there for the day.

Once we had settled in, and Troy had gotten ready to head back to the bar for another day of work, we took turns taking showers. The heat of the water, and the gentleness of the mist as it hit my face reminded me of coming in from a long winter walk, the flowery shampoo and conditioner made my hair feel soft and supple, the razor against my warm, wet skin as I shaved my legs went smoothly unlike the combination of the cold water, and soap that I had been rubbing on my legs as I shaved them over the sink in gas station bathrooms. My skin felt tight, and I stood under the warmth of the water until my fingers and toes were pruney. At first the water that trickled down my body was a dark, muddy colour—we had only had chances to wash our hands and faces, and wipe down the rest of our bodies while at the safe house, and on the road—and by the time I was finished my skin squeaked when I rubbed my fingers against it. I felt renewed. When we had all showered, Emilie went back to sleep and Gary and I spent the day drinking tea, snacking on fresh vegetables and fruits, and taking advantage of the access to satellite television and internet. The video campaign was successful online—as soon as authorities had taken it down from one site, it popped up on another, and back on the first one after only a few minutes. From what we could tell by the news broadcasts it had reached parts of Asia, most of Europe, South America, wealthier parts of Africa, all of Oceania, and had been played on every news network in the United States. There were reports of increases in gun and ammunitions sales. People were either angry or afraid, and neither one of those was good for the current political leaders.

The RCMP began setting up checkpoints along highways, to search all vehicles passing by for firearms and ammunition, the only province that wouldn't put up with it was Alberta; Albertans are like Texans, they know their rights, and they wouldn't stand for the violation thereof. We knew that we would have to move onto the next phase of our plan in Winnipeg, and we would need Troy's help to get it done. We had little time left to get to Alberta. When Emilie woke up it was already 3 pm, we forced her to eat and drink while we explained what was happening, and tried to get her to pull out of the fog of the previous night. We were desperate. We needed to move quickly. It didn't take her long to go and get Troy to come back. We spent the rest of the evening, and into the night going over the plans, and figuring out the details. It was midnight before we reached the beds, which were pillow soft and warm; for the first time since leaving the cabin we were truly comfortable.

AN END

There was a loud rapping at the front door, and we jumped out of the bed, quickly threw on our clothes, and prepared ourselves to run as fast as our wobbly legs would take us. Troy walked down the hall, his steps were light, but quick, the door creaked as he opened it, Gary held my right hand in his left, and our bags in his right. The door shut, and Troy knocked on our door. We opened. "It was a delivery guy. There's a package for us. It's probably something from Aunty." Gary let go of my hand, and the blood rushed to my fingers. Troy went back to his room and woke Emilie, and we sat down with coffee and bagels, staring at the package in the middle of the kitchen table. Wondering what it could be, and what we would like for it to be. That's when I felt it, the first inkling of movement, an involuntary smile crept across my face, and I closed my eyes to focus on that movement. It had been a week since I had seen the doctor, and I had so many questions, so many worries, but all of those washed away with those first flits of activity. Gary sat down and opened up the package. It wasn't from Lucille, there was a note attached with no signature that read —*I hope this helps*—

Emilie grabbed the box and pulled out what looked like a map of some sort just from the sheer size of it. She unfolded it and carefully laid it out on the floor; it was the blueprints for Parliament Hill. It was exactly what we needed. The blueprints showed a series of underground tunnels which were generally unarmed, and would allow for one of us to get into the offices of the Prime Minister and her cabinet, and do what needed to be done. It was decided for me that I would stay behind and wait because of "your condition." It was Emilie's way of avoiding saying baby. It would be another week before we would be able to accomplish our goal, but that gave us plenty of time to prepare, to organize activist groups, distribute flyers calling for mass protest, to create distractions that would ensure that those who needed to be in their offices would be there, and that those that needed to be far away would be occupied by unruly student groups, and protestors. We were setting the stage for our first major Act, and we made sure that it would go off without a hitch. The Monday before we struck was Thanksgiving, but it went unobserved that year; most families had experienced too much loss in the past two years to be thankful for anything. We worked together to make a ham dinner with mashed potatoes, gravy, and roasted vegetables, Gary and I made an apple-cranberry pie, and we feasted off of paper plates while going over the final draft of our plan. Gary, Emilie, and Troy would leave the house at 7 a.m. and would arrive on Parliament Hill by 8 a.m. They would each have their backpack with leaflets, water, a small snack, mask, and the piece de resistance. Protestors would be piling onto the Hill as early as they could get there, so they would be able to sneak past security. They would give us plenty of time, and cover to make it towards the openings for the tunnels. They would have until 11 a.m. to navigate through the tunnels and make it inside the offices. The Prime Minister would be in her office, we had left instruction with a militia group to strike right at 11:00 a.m., and they would provide the first distraction of many. In her office, the Prime Minister would be considered safe and accounted for, at that time Emilie would make her way inside her office, Gary would take on the Governor General, and Troy would keep watch—he had brawn that Gary could only dream of having. Once they made their way in, they would call me. Lastly, I would read the script that we had agreed upon with Lucille and the others. We were to be the first ones to strike, the other teams would wait for us, and they then would follow suit in their assigned regions. The goal was to force immediate shutdowns of government with little to no losses, imposing an impromptu government of our peers for no more than three months. Things never go as planned.

There is an old cliché about how history is written by those who are victorious, that's why I'm here, that is why I am writing this for you. When they arrived at Parliament Hill, the plaza was packed with protestors, and many of them had already begun to get violent near the back of the crowds. The Police presence was higher than what we had expected, but then again so was the sheer number of protestors. Some people had brought along their children, and I would never understand why. Maybe they thought things could be resolved peacefully, perhaps they were just convinced that Canadians would never riot; after all, our Nation had projected an image of peace and conflict-free resolution for decades. When they arrived, Gary decided that they would be quicker, and most likely more efficient if they split up; he would take his chances along the Eastern entrances, Troy would make his way along the tunnels, and Emilie would maneuver through the West gates. As they pushed through the crowd, they would randomly throw leaflets into the air, hoping that this would distract not only the protesters into gathering into clusters to grab at the papers dancing down towards the ground, but also that those forming clusters would cause the Police to take interest, and move away from the barricades. What Gary hadn't anticipated, was that other protesters would notice their breaking through the barricades, and follow. As soon as they were able to sneak beyond the boundaries onto the still green lawns in front of the Parliament building, someone from within the crowd shouted something inaudible over the hum of the other thousands of voices, and a wave of bodies began to plow forward. It reminded me of when I would sit in the window seat as a little girl watching the snow plow come down the road, the snow piling up and spilling over in what seemed like a giant white wave. I could barely make out the three little specs running across the grass towards the back buildings, when the first explosion came. It seemed so surreal, almost cartoon like. The bodies of men, women, even children, flew through the air and the cries of mothers rang out like church bells at a wedding. My heart sank, but there was no turning back, no undoing what had happened. Within moments of the first explosion, military personnel filed in, and began shooting, they were met with pipe bombs, and militiamen with military grade rifles. Some of those that came there to protest peacefully were able to leave, some even managed to make it out with their own children, or with children whose parents had been blown into a thousand indistinguishable pieces of mangled flesh. That's when the call came in. Gary, Troy, and Emilie had made it into the building, planted the surveillance cameras, and come into contact with the Governor General and Prime Minister. It was my turn, I now had to take responsibility for the riot that was taking place.

"Good morning!" My tone was strong, exactly as I had rehearsed it over and over again, "As you can see, the People are unhappy. I organized them, I brought them here, it was MY voice, MY message to retaliate, to force change that awakened them!" I paused, my hands were shaking, I was nervous, I was afraid, and I was heartbroken. "My friends have some documents for you," Another pause, my mouth was becoming dry, and I felt ill. "You will sign the first set of documents, Madam Prime Minister, you will be effectively shutting down the government of Canada. This first document calls for a Tabula Rasa, if you will. All services, except for health care and financial services that benefit Canadians—CPP, CCTB, etc.—will stop immediately, all Members of the House and Senate will be discharged of their duties without severance, and without their pensions. Madame Governor General, your signature will do what it always does, it will give the Queen's seal of approval…"

"There is no way in HELL that I am going to sign this shit. Who the fuck do you think you are?!? I am the goddamned Prime Minister, you hear me?!?" Her voice screeched through the phone. I waited patiently for her to finish spewing her lies, and her self-righteous diatribe. "Are you quite finished?!?" My patience was wearing thin, and she had wasted enough of my time. "Now, would you both please sign the document, the country is watching." The cameras were connected to one of the many proxy servers that the hackers used to keep their location untraceable, and they would be working hard to make sure that this was being seen live across Canada, and Internationally. They were dumbfounded, and the Prime Minister started blushing intensely for her rant. They picked up their pens and signed the documents. "Well, then. Now that you two are no longer representing this nation that I love dearly, please take yourselves down to the lobby, and surrender yourselves for crimes which violate the Constitution and the Bill of Rights and Freedoms, as well as several International laws. There are members of the RCMP waiting for you, and a crowd that is more than ready, and more than happy to judge you on the spot." The fear that fell upon their faces was a sight that I had been waiting to see since the beginning of the attacks. "Or, you can choose to look at the other set of documents that my friends have brought with them. These documents are a kind of confession; by signing these papers you will be admitting that the Nuclear strike on Beijing two years ago, and every other related attack, has been part and partial to a global strategy at dissolving individual governments by causing populations to dwindle rapidly, economies to suffer drastically, and give people no other option but to consent to the formation of a singular governing body which would heavily police and constrain the rights of individuals. This document also details which governments were in agreement to this plan, and played a crucial role in its enactment. Furthermore, in signing this document, you agree to formally testify and provide all supporting evidence, including private correspondence between yourself and any other person. Oh, and one last thing. You will never be able to work in any way for any government body again. Do you consent? Or, would you prefer the crowd outside your doors to decide your fate, much like your government has decided the fates of millions of poor and downtrodden?"

They were dumbfounded, but without a moment's hesitation they signed. I thanked them, and let them know that they were free to go home. When Gary, Emilie, and Troy returned it was late in the evening. They had to be creative in how they weaseled their way around the bloodshed. "So, it's done." Gary looked at me. "Yeah." It was the only answer I could find. The blood of those people was on our hands, we had become like the thing we hated most: A corrupt institution.

NEW BEGINNINGS

The riots continued in Winnipeg, thousands of people traveled from all over in order to join in; major cities were facing immediate shutdowns and restructurings, big businesses were being burned to the ground, and their Presidents and CEO's across the country were getting a piece of their just desserts; except it didn't feel like justice to me. Troy and Emilie decided to head back to Toronto to deliver the documents to Lucille, and Gary and I were done. We had accomplished our tasks. We drove straight through to Alberta, the new van was a gift from Lucille, and we kept it as a reminder of who we had been, of what we had done, and where we had travelled. The sale on my father's house had never been finalized, so it stood empty, waiting for me to take over caring for it. It had never stopped being home. When we drove up to the big empty house, with all of the memories packed into tight corners, waiting to explode out into the atmosphere, and renew the image of my family that I had carried away with me, a feeling of wholeness washed over me. We spent the rest of the winter months, and into the spring preparing our home; we pulled out all of the old baby furniture from the attic, and cleaned away the smell of rotting flesh that had been trapped in the house since my father's death.

The nuclear bombs kept falling, all of the major cities were wiped out, and people began to wander aimlessly through the expanse of burning, rotting wastelands. Eventually all contact was lost between countries, and it was assumed that we were all that was left. Satellites were destroyed, so communication between countries would be nearly impossible to resume. Despite everything that was going on in the world, we knew that we would be safe in our Alberta home. At least, as long as we could maintain our sovereignty. Gary and I liked the idea of returning to a bartering system, a simple way of life where you lived off the land you had, and you traded with your neighbours for the things that you didn't have and couldn't make. But, people were desperate for stability, stability that they thought could only come from a single governing body—a group of elected officials to tell them what was right and wrong—and the group that had we worked for had a ready solution.

My pregnancy went smoothly, and despite all of the radiation that I had been exposed to the doctor was certain you'd be fine. One morning, only a month before you were born, I was cleaning out my father's old desk and found a key that will lead us to discover something great together. You were born into a tumultuous time. The day that you were born was the day that the new government was announced, and the migrations started. I never thought it would have been possible for things to turn so quickly, for life to feel so normal.

End Part I

PART II

GROWING

I never understood why she went on and on about the war. It had turned out okay; we had our home in Alberta, the Oil companies stopped drilling, the snow stopped falling a grayish-brown, and regained its whiteness by the time I was twelve. We worked hard, and the first five years of my life were anything but easy. Banks had closed down, the entire market system had crashed, and nation after nation fell into civil war. Canada was first, which mother always said was surprising to her, she had always assumed Canadians to be pacifists. I was just a baby when the United States fell, and millions of their citizens migrated to the Rocky Mountains for safety; it was the only place that we could be safe from the radiation that poured over the earth. The closer you could get to the Rockies the better off you were, but that safety wasn't guaranteed, nor did it last for long. The nuclear storms would pass through the mountains just as they had the plains, the deserts, the tundra and the oceans. There wasn't a speck of Earth that hadn't been violated by Man's greed, and politics. After the fall of Parliament, with the emergence of nuclear strikes all over the world, and growing unrest in the Eastern Provinces, the Northwest Territories, Yukon, and Nunavut broke off from Canada, and formed their own alliance—they would eventually return to the traditional Inuit way of life—and it was decided that a safe haven would be established in the West.

Banff became a center for immigration. It was one of the few Canadian places that Americans were acutely aware of. The others, mother would add, were Calgary for its Stampede and Oil and Gas operations, and Toronto for just about everything else. Millions of Americans would stop in Banff and register as refugees, and even Easterners migrated westward to avoid the nuclear fallout for as long as they could. The fish in the seas were dying out, and the fishing trade became a bad word. Western Canada had plenty of fisheries, ranches, chicken farms, and crop farms, and British Colombia was always ripe with Orchards, so food supply wasn't a concern. Canadians had always understood the importance of a central government system for the benefit of keeping order. Mother used to regale me with stories of large hospitals, where women would go to give birth, and how proud she had been when she gave birth to me at home in the bathtub filled with warm water. After the initial shutdown there were no hospitals that were operating safely, so she decided that she would do it herself.

"You came earlier than we had expected," she would tell me as we kneaded the dough for our special WinterMas bread "but I didn't let that put any fear into my heart, I had your father fill the tub with nice hot water, and I spent twelve hours in there, with my back feeling like it was on fire, and my entire body wanting to collapse in on itself. The pain of giving birth told me that I was doing well, the contractions were a clear sign that you were ready, that I was ready; even if your father wasn't." She always laughed about how he had almost fainted when I had started crowning, but her laughter would always turn into a soft smile as she recalled how he wept on the bathroom floor when I finally emerged from her body, and swam to the top for my first breath.

She would wake up early on Sunday mornings, quickly slip out of bed to start on breakfast. When they were ready she'd put the placki with jam and simulated hot chocolate beverage on a bed tray and take them up to him. With her foot gently pushing the door open, mother would almost sing his name, then place the tray on his bedside table and waft the steam towards him. She would then come and pull me out of bed, gently rubbing my back and calling me to wake. We would sit, eating our placki and drinking the chocolate drink until Papa came down in his robe and slippers. He would hum old hymns as he sat in his chair reading paper books; a rare and expensive hobby.

When I was younger people would call on Papa to ask his opinion about policies to safeguard the future. He too had been instrumental in bringing about the revolution, and he was well educated, so his opinion was worth gold to the new policymakers, and he was happy to give it. My parents became integral to establishing the new order of things; they would do everything they could to ensure that there were equal opportunities for everyone, so we packed up our things, and moved into the Centre, where we lived in a bright, beautiful cabin. The outside was log, and seemed unimpressive, but when you stepped through the thick wooden door the largesse of the space could overwhelm you. The ceilings were deceptively high, the rooms were large and furnished with the most expensive, and stylish wares: the chesterfield, chairs, and benches were all leather and chrome, the tables and counters were made of marble and shale with dark cherry paneling, the light fixtures were precious crystal and silver and sparkled like a clear night sky, astounding art hung around the room, and mirrors reflected the opalescence of the space. The stairwell leading upstairs towards the bedrooms and offices wound around an ancient totem pole, and the bedrooms were outfitted as decadently as the main floor. The cottage had once belonged to a member of the old regime, he had built it to be suitable as a winter vacation home for himself and his wife. I ran into the bedroom that had been obviously set up for a girl, and jumped onto the soft bed which was covered in the sleekest silk comforter and piled with down pillows; for the first few days I pinned posters and photographs to my walls, unpacked my clothes and books, but after that I spent a lot of my time skiing, and hiking until the school year commenced. The mountains were always beaming with new life, and they were the only place where I felt whole. My mother once told me that my grandfather had been that way too. My peers always expected me to have an opinion about policies that were being passed daily, but I never took interest in my father's work, and my mother spent her days reading stories, and trying to write her own, something which hardly piqued my curiosity.

My parents didn't allow me to watch government footage, even though my friends did, but I didn't mind. My life was carefree, and I was allowed to come and go as I pleased so long as my schoolwork never suffered. Our life there was good. We could study if we wanted to, we could walk around with liberty, say what we were thinking, and we could shop whenever we wanted. We had currency, but it was nothing so primitive as the paper and plastic that my parents had been accustomed to. We were the test group for the identification chips that are now inserted at birth; our chips were placed two inches above our wrists in our forearm and they contained our personal identification—name, date of birth, place of birth, current dwelling locus, DNA sequence, and credit information. The technology was unsophisticated, and had to be changed every two years, but it was a staunch improvement over what had previously been considered innovative technology. As more people migrated in, running away from the wastelands that were dominating the rest of the world, The Centre expanded, the buildings were built tall—some as high as 150 stories—and the architecture was breathtaking. As precious as Copper was, there was no expense too great, no material too extravagant to create the presidential palace. The streets were rebuilt with marble and shale mined from nearby mountains, and the city sparkled. There would be nights when mother and papa would argue.

"What's the use, Gary? Did we really go through

all of that, and sacrifice those lives in Winnipeg for this? It's no better; in fact it is the exact same bullshit! The ONLY difference is that other than fighting this Aristocratic shit, we have become part of it!" When I would peak out of my bedroom at the top of the stairs, the light peering in from the living room, she would be standing—or pacing—in the middle of the room ringing her hands, her hair hanging loosely down her back, tears filling her eyes.

"What are we supposed to do, Dani? I've tried talking to the council, I've reasoned with the policy makers, other than killing them off, and anyone else who share their sentiments, there are no more options!" His forehead would glisten with sweat, and his hands would flail in every direction. Papa never yelled, but his tone was passionate and strong, his brow would furrow, and he would run his fingers through his thick silvering hair. He had always found the constant banter between himself and the elected officials, and the bickering he endured at home overwhelming. They would only argue once I had gone to bed, but it didn't stop me from hearing them. As I got older, all I wanted to do was get away, to stay away from that house. I didn't understand why mother was so incensed; we had a good and comfortable life. What more could she want?

As the population grew tunnels were built into the mountains to allow for storage of goods, quick travel, and refuge from attacks even though we were certain that the rest of the world was a rotting wasteland. In time the Canadian Pacific Railway was rebuilt towards the East, and wards were established. The wards came together almost on their own; as the Science Department determined that soil was safe and water as drinkable people began to travel back east. Once it was determined that the prairies were safe to return to, and farm, and that the mines, and forests in what was once Saskatchewan and Manitoba were hospitable, hoards of families moved out in their direction to find work, and raise families, with hope of bright, wealthy futures. New towns were established every few months, and the maps had to be re-drawn constantly as fault lines shifted, and nuclear runoff began accumulating in certain areas. We had lost touch with Europe, Asia, and Africa after only a year; I was only a newborn when the last broadcast was detected from London, and the message was clear that England, and all of Europe had come under a giant nuclear storm—it was unlikely that anyone could have survived. There was some comfort in knowing that we were alone, that there were no other enemies waiting to take over what we had built. As the clouds, and reactions came fewer, and with more time in between them, we all began to relax, to simply enjoy the new life, the new society that we had begun to create. When I was seventeen the Taktikhause met together with the mayors, and elected representatives of each ward—which were still unofficial and constantly fighting over boundaries—to address the issues of ward borders, goods and services distribution, taxation, and inalienable rights. They had decided that it was best to designate each ward by its most valuable natural resource. There was the Fishing ward which was called "Samaki", which mostly consisted of fisheries, since the ocean was too toxic to allow for any boating, let alone fishing. The Orchard ward which after a long voting process decided upon the name "Frugthave", their borders would run along the Rocky mountain range into the interior of what was British Columbia where the Orchards and berry farms were already well established. The traditional crop and husbandry district, which easily decided on "Fattoria", was one of the largest wards and its borders expanded through what had been the Southern Alberta prairies, Southern Saskatchewan and into the Dakotas. Forestry, though less necessary with the invention of stronger, more durable plastic and metal infusions, had a large boundary that overtook what had been Northern British Colombia, and the Yukon, was named "Stejar". Although the reserves were low, and my father fought vehemently against its use, the Oil sands were put back into production and the small ward surrounding them was given the name "Nafta", there would be more over the years to come, but these were the most important for our society to be able to succeed and expand.

I had always been aware that life outside of the valley would have been challenging; the landscape was often difficult to navigate, roads had been demolished by protestors, some springs and wells had become toxic, and there was no way for travelers to tell which were safe and which would lead to death; so they would carry jugs of purified water in their caravans. Once reports began trickling in of travelers dying in the wilderness from animal attacks, hunger, thirst, injury, or misjudging the landscape, the "Travelers Bill" was introduced and signed. It stipulated that all those wishing to travel must do so with a permit and that they must travel by aircraft until a safe land travel method could be implemented. This also made it easier to keep track of the population as it spread out into the wards. Mother wanted desperately to return, and with the pension that father would receive, and the stipend that mother had been given for her role in the "global economic change" as the textbooks called it, we could have lived as comfortably as was possible out in Nafta. Papa, on the other hand, was reluctant to leave the safety of the Centre; he would come home some evenings with a worried look on his face, and when I was seemingly out of earshot, and they felt they could speak more freely he would take mother's hands, tenderly, and rest his head against her chest and weep. He would tell her of the messages that reached his office of entire families being slaughtered over a few feet of land, and of crops that would fail because the soil was still too laden with fission particles. The thing that devastated him the most was stories of young families who gave birth to stillborn babies, or worse babies with severe deformities that would often die after only a few days, and those that would survive would have to navigate through life with physical deformities, and mental and developmental retardation. Physicians were scarce in the wards, most preferred to stay in the Centre where they felt safe, and where their services were often paid for privately and not out of the public coffers, so the children would only see a nurse for a few weeks after delivery, and to receive their routine vitamin injections, and then the family would have to either pay for private nursing to help with raising their child, or barter for the services of an apothecary for medicines, and decide the rest on their own. Papa feared that I would suffer the same fate as the other couples did, and he secretly hoped that I would never marry, and never have children. He agreed that once he was ready to retire, when he finally felt either that he had been victorious, or that he had been completely defeated with no chance for reform, that we would return to mother's childhood home, the one that I was born into.

I had no desire to leave the Centre; it had become a part of me, and the landscape beckoned me to stay. Papa retired shortly after my seventeenth birthday, and we waited for me to finish the school year, and decide upon my further education, before moving back. The cabin would always be ours to own, and so when I had decided to stay in the Centre so that I could attend the Centre University for Higher Studies, my parents left me the keys to the house, and recommended that I get roommates. They left for Nafta in mid-August when the sun was at its highest, and the dirt was hot as embers. The stillness of the August air was stifling that year, and I spent most of my time keeping cool in the designated pools, and doing my pre-reading for my first term of classes in Biology and Kinesiology. Many of my friends decided to stay behind and pursue their studies, because, like me, they had no desire to move to one of the wards as was required for all of those who were able bodied, and were not pursuing further education to do. Hundreds of our classmates were shipped out to various wards to find employment, and if the Taktikhause had its way, fall in love, and settle down; the majority did by the time they had reached the age of twenty-one. The thought of falling in love never did not cross my mind, nor did the idea of leaving my carefree life behind and starting a proper family, and it gave me a lot of comfort knowing that I had made the right choice.

Housing in the Centre became limited for students, so labourers were brought in from the wards and worked tirelessly from sunrise to sunset building tall towers, with relatively simply furnished units for students of the University, and more grandly devised towers for licensed and employed citizens of the Centre. The labourers were not permitted to go out into the local night scene to meet young women, as the Taktikhause feared that they might ruin the chances of the bright young Central women at gaining a successful career that would lead to greater prosperity for the whole nation. There were few students from outside of the Centre that would attend University, most young people, regardless of their intelligence or potential, were required to remain in their ward because they were most desperately needed there to help with the local industry, but there was an exception made each year for a handful who scored miraculously on the entrance exams. Even though they would receive an education in the Centre, and they had the pleasure of experiencing all that life had to offer there, most of them returned to their Wards. Some would return as physicians, and charge apothecary rates; others would return as engineers and help their ward design better and safer building, and equipment for industrial use, many of the young women who made it into the Centre would return with better knowledge of reproduction, and would be able to help safely deliver babies, and help new parents better care for their infants. They were rewarded handsomely with an annual gift from the Taktikhause.

As winter approached and the bright lights

would adorn the evergreens, and shiny baubles would reflect through windows, each household received a letter and a small package from the Minister. The package was empty, but the letter asked that each house fill it with tokens that would bring a little joy and hope to children and families in the wards for the Winter Feast Days. I filled mine with a certificate to the local market for fresh vegetables, fruits, and meat for a WinterMas feast, a certificate to be taken to the clothing warehouse for whatever it is that they could need, a small doll, some coloured pencils, notebooks, and games. The old woman who worked at the post office, smiled gently at me, and I couldn't help but wonder why. "You know," her voice was raspy and thick for her small frame "when I was a little girl in the late 1970's we would participate in something similar to this; we would fill shoeboxes with fun games, colouring books, toothbrushes, and sewing kits and then we would wrap the shoeboxes in paper with mistletoe, stockings, or Santa printed on it, and it would be sent off to some far away country where children were starving, and had no hope for an education." Her smile faded as quickly as it had come on, and there was a profound sadness in her face. I didn't understand why she found it so sad that this small tradition was being carried on. Her eyes shot up and she looked straight into mine as she read my chip. Her hands were rough, dry, and calloused from years of hard work, and her face was befitted with deep wrinkles that captured her every emotion; her bright white hair framed her face in a cascade of perfect curls, and her teeth sparkled as she smiled and bid me a good day. She was beautiful and complex, and I knew she had been strong throughout her life.

    I spent the rest of that evening trying to imagine what it would have been like to grow up in a time period that didn't have the Internet, and where you had to leave your house for the smallest of conveniences. It was strange to me, the idea that in order to see a friend I would have to leave the comfort of my home, when all I had to do was tell my chip to find the friend I wished to see, and within moments their hologram would be standing in front of me. How she must have felt when she could witness so many great historical events; events that led to this post-nuclear paradise. I had read a lot of old books about how people imagined a nuclear war would leave the Earth, or how people would have to band together into primitive tribes in order to survive; those authors would have been surprised at what we had managed to rebuild in only twenty years. The University itself was a haven for art and architecture. The halls leading from amphitheatre to amphitheatre were lined with beautiful student made pieces; the mess hall was domed with embossed porcelain ceiling tiles, which contrasted against the rough, unpolished gray marble table tops, with white glass pedestal feet resting on bright red glass bricks. The red was like that of the sun as it set over the mountain tops, and the sky would turn an eerie blood orange with sweeps of pink and purple, and would bring to mind the bruises that would spread over my knees, palms, and shins after having bailed down a hill, my foot almost always having had tripped up over a tree root, or a muddy patch. It brought with it a reminder that the earth was still healing, even though we had already rebuilt so much.

Reluctorad shelters, we called them Relies, were one of the first scientific innovations that scientists worked on once people had started migrating to the Centre; it was a dangerous process that required alloys to be sent out into known nuclear hotspots, with some poor rodent trapped inside, then retrieved after forty-eight hours and tested for how much radiation managed to find its way in through the alloy. Reluctorad was the final product. There hadn't been any nuclear storms in the Centre for at least fifteen years at that point, and most of the Relies were being used to store grains, medical supplies, and emergency relief packages, and the ones that were left open, were always in vogue for parties.

I didn't often go to parties, I always preferred the company of a quiet book and a cozy comforter, to the raucous of a party, so it came as quite a shock to my friend Zyrene when I had agreed to let her throw me a party for my twenty-first birthday. She had gone to a lot of trouble to plan a party for me, so I had to put on a good show for our friends—most of whom I hardly knew, but they knew her, and so they would come and eat, and drink, and dance, and wish me a "Happy Birthday, and only the best that currency can yield!" It was an odd salutation, but it was appropriate for a Central girl like me. Even though I had always felt most at home in the Centre, with its fine dining, the University, the countless stores and seamstresses, and endless entertainment, I never truly felt a part of the culture. I enjoyed the shopping, and the picture houses, the art galleries, and virtual museums, the salons, the spas, the eateries, but what I loved most of all was my hiking boots, plaid shirts, and the smell of the woods when I would leave the noise behind me, and enter into the wilderness behind the cabin. I suppose I craved the adventure, the exhilaration of knowing that I could find myself up against some feral creature, some undiscovered mutation of a bear, or coyote, or that I could simply fall, hit my head, and never be found again. Perhaps the most exhilarating thought was that of getting lost, of never being able to get back to the shallow, to the polite, to the "always on" air that the men and women who lived in the Centre carried with them.

Zyrene was unlike me; she was dark and tall, her voice was thick and sultry, she always knew what to say and how to stand, her clothes were stylish, and her skin was flawless. Her eyes were a deep chocolate brown, and sparkled in the most unusual way—she always claimed it was a mutation from all of the radiation that her mother was exposed to when she was pregnant with Zyrene when the bombs first started to fall. Zyrene walked with confidence, and she was very much a socialite. She sat on the couch with a glass of Sauvignon Blanc in her right hand, and a private entry card in her left; she was flipping the card between her fingers, her ankles crossed, and her blue lace appliqué dress just barely hiding her crotch, and her perfect breasts clearly visible in the right light, with her long, slender legs beautifully accented by a pair of off kilter yellow heels. I stepped out of my room wearing my simple yellow dress, which cinched at the waist then flared out at a forty five degree angle until it hit the middle of my thighs. The top of my dress was embellished by small crystals all along the deep sweetheart neckline, and outlining my bust, my shoulders were bare and my toes poked out from my ruby red pumps. Zyrene quickly pulled my hair into a pristine twist, and painted my face to give me a more polished appearance. "Mmm, you look stunning babe!" She flicked her thin wrist "Alright, let's get a chauf and we can arrive in style and on time." I always felt a little slow witted when I was around her. "Okay." I was nervous, and my hands began to shake. "Here," she handed me a small pill "Take this. It'll calm you right down. You've got nothin' to worry 'bout, baby girl." She passed me a glass of wine. "Oh, I'll be alright. I really don't think I should take that." I handed her the pill back, and swung back the wine. It was bitter, and my jaw tightened from the tartness of it. I had always preferred dessert wines.

NEW ADVENTURES

My parents came the next morning, and took me out for a birthday brunch. A meal that my mother loved, because "You get all the best parts of breakfast and lunch in one meal."; Papa, on the other hand, preferred his meals to be separated by a mid-morning snack, so brunch confused him and he never knew what to order. "So," Papa began awkwardly "how are things with the cabin?" I looked up from my scrambled eggs, and hash browns "Fine. I had the chimney swept by one of the Wardsmen; I overheard him talking about needing to send home money for the baby's medicine. How are things at the house in Albertsford?"

"Oh just fine," mother chimed in as she tore her croissant, and spread the marmalade "the roof needs fixing, but we're going to have our neighbours do that. They're a young family, and could use the extra income and tutoring for their children. How are things at the University? Are they still spreading that crap propaganda as history?" Papa stopped in the middle of his bite of Eggs Benedict, and shot her a look that I'd never seen from him before. He was angry with her, and there was fear in his eyes. I rolled my eyes. After brunch, we went back to the cabin, built a fire, and enjoyed a glass of wine as we discussed all of the books I had been reading, and my thoughts on the politics of the time—sixteenth century authors were some of my favourites, and their politics screamed loudly at me. It was a Saturday, and they had intended on staying the night. Zyrene agreed to stay at her boyfriend's for the night, and I set up her room for my parents. Papa insisted on making a pot roast for dinner, even though I had planned on Salmon. "Beef is more economical, Marie. Not to mention the farmed Salmon is nowhere near as good as the Wild Salmon that your mother and I used to eat." I hated it when my parents compared what we had now to what they had enjoyed before the war. Before they went to bed mother presented me with a package.

The paper it was wrapped in was embossed with golden leaves, and there was a letter attached to it.

Marie,

I know it's been difficult growing up in this world, in the shadow of parents who were both instrumental in bringing about this change—not all of which your Papa and I are particularly happy about. Nonetheless, I hope that you know we always had your best interest in mind, and that we truly have done the best that we can with what we have. I need you to understand the truth about how things came about, and of how the world turned upside down overnight. Your winter break is almost over, but I hope that you can find some time to sit down and read through all of this, and I hope that it helps you to understand why I've spent so much of my life just poring over manuscripts that my father had been given to "edit". I love you dearly.

Mama

My curiosity was peaked, and I couldn't help

but tear into the beautiful paper. Inside I found a large leather-bound notebook, and as I flipped the pages I could detect the smells of my childhood; mother's perfume, papa's cologne, the subtle scent of lilacs which she would bring in and place in vases throughout the house, the aroma of goulash and bigos came off of the pages, and that's how I would know that she had penned those around WinterMas. Some of the pages had rings from glasses of wine, and cups of tea, the early pages had remnants of coffee and chocolate; mother had told me that in her youth she had drunk coffee daily, and could have chocolate at any moment, but now it was a rare treat. Attached to the back cover was a key; it was made of brass, and dangled on a small silver chain. At first I thought it was a joke; that she had to have some better gift for me, after all a twenty-first birthday is a milestone, but mother wasn't one to play practical jokes. The Epilogue to this notebook full of mysteries and truths was simply "I know it doesn't look like much, and frankly I have no idea what it opens, but that's the gift; we can discover it together. Find the lock that fits the key, it'll be our adventure!" I wasn't certain what to think of it. It was my final year at University, and I was on track to become a Conservateur—I would be able to spend most of my days in the woods, and up into the mountain ranges as far out as the Northern-most borders, studying wildlife, and avoiding humanity—so our adventure would have to wait until after I had graduated; something which mother was perfectly aware of.

My parents had always gotten used to waking up at sunrise, so they let me sleep, and had let themselves out; they needed to be home by nine in order to get things started with the roof. I woke up to the smell of cinnamon buns, and coffee, so I jumped out of my bed, still in my red lace panties and white tank top, ran down the stairs to find the house empty; papa had put on an old blues record which he had brought with him, so the house was filled with the sound of New York in the early twentieth century. I had always known that my childhood home was filled with treasures that others could only ever dream of, and this had always been one of my favourites. I spent the morning reading the manuscript that mother had given me; I was discovering a woman that I had never known, a woman that was adventurous, generous, giving, fearless, sexual, and at times completely lost in her forward motion. It never occurred to me that I was reading my mother's story, because the woman that she had written seemed so far removed from the woman I had known my entire life, and it was this version of her that I wanted to know. The second term of my final year of studies went by quickly, and I graduated with highest honours for my senior thesis on the effects of sub-molecular radiation clusters in rotting brush. I received the Greenwood fellowship award for my innovative methodology and critical approach to a subject that was generally undervalued, and rarely studied. My parents were proud, as any parent would be, and they took me out to dinner after the convocation. I wanted to ask her about the book, but I wasn't sure when it would be appropriate to breech the subject, or how to even bring it up—I had completely forgotten about the key. We spent the evening talking about my research, about my plans for the future, and about the possibility of leaving the Centre. It was their desire that I go with them, but I had a job lined up with the Department of Health and Natural Regrowth to continue my research. It was a rare opportunity and I didn't want to pass it up. My new Social Bracket Status was scheduled to be updated from Student: Funds Limited to Parental Income Level G (15%), to Employed: Single Female Income Level D, two weeks after graduation; it was an entry level position, but one with prestige, and a significant amount of pay. It was rare for students to be hired for a Government position right out of University, and when it did happen, it generally meant that they would advance quickly and head up their department within ten years, so long as they didn't make any controversial political alliances or statements. It was difficult on researchers, because they had to be tactful in addressing societal practices as being detrimental to a positive outcome, but it was possible to present solutions for things that could detrimentally affect the natural surroundings without causing any social or political backlash. If papa had taught me anything about politics, it was tact; something which mother lacked.

"Well," mother wiped her mouth with the white

napkin, and placed her fork and knife on her plate "that was delicious! Should we get some dessert?" She gently placed the napkin back on her lap, and sipped on her wine.

"Sure." Papa was never one to pass up something sweet. "How about a slice of cheesecake?" Strawberry was his favourite, and he would get a cup of tea to balance the sweetness of it.

"Cheesecake sounds good." I looked across the table at them, they were still very much in love, and they held hands whenever possible. "So, mom?" I was nervous "I read that manuscript you gave me."

"Oh?" There was an excitement in her eyes, and a desperate need for me to have understood it the way that she had meant for it to be understood.

"Yeah," I breathed in deeply, my palms were beginning to sweat "I um…." The waiter came up to the table.

"You're all done with the main course, I see." He scanned our faces "Can I get you some dessert? Another drink?"

"Oh, yes," papa chimed in "Three Strawberry

cheesecakes and teas please." The waiter smiled agreeably, his teeth were pearl white, and his skin was a beautiful olive colour, his eyes sparkled green like the nearby lakes, and his hair was as black as the soot that lined the fireplace.

"You were saying?" Mother looked at me imploringly. She made me nervous.

"Yeah, it was really well written, and I had never heard things told from that perspective before. You should publish it." It came out like a stream of vitriol, and I couldn't stop it. I knew it was awful, and not at all what she wanted me to say, but it was all that I could muster.

"Well," she swallowed hard, and smiled at the waiter as he brought about our cheesecake, "I'm glad you enjoyed it. What about the adventure that I proposed at the end? The key?" There was anticipation in her voice, and I could see how anxious she was for me to answer.

"Oh, that." I wasn't certain how to answer her, I hadn't thought much about it. "Well, I start work in two weeks, so maybe we could, I don't know, try and find that lock while I wait to get started." I couldn't believe that I had said that, that I had proposed that she and I go off on our own,, just the two of us, alone. Our relationship had always been tense, and we never quite knew what to say to one another. When I was quite small she was very good with me; we would spend hours upon hours playing with dolls, colouring in books, she taught me letters and numbers, and how to spell as soon as I was able to speak decently. It was when I got older; around the time that I turned fifteen that she started to become distant. That was also when she and papa started to fight about policies that the Taktikhause had begun to propose; policies that no one was supposed to be aware of in the public. I think that is when the key became a burden for her, she was beginning to feel restless about what was locked away, about what her father had hidden, and not even told her or his lawyers about.

"Oh wonderful!" She clapped her hands together, and sat up like a puppy that had just been given a reward for good behavior, "We'll get ourselves all packed up tomorrow, and set out on Monday!" She looked over at papa, and smiled brightly. I knew that this was the opportunity that we needed to connect, to get to know each other, and to understand each others' thinking, but the idea of being alone with her for two weeks was overwhelming.

We spent all of Saturday shopping for supplies and packing. It had been a long time since mother travelled anywhere, and she was beaming with excitement. There was an inkling of the woman that she had written about, as we looked for proper footwear, and hiking packs. "Did dziadek leave any clues?" I asked her as we tried on big, comfortable boots. "Just a few little things that I was able to find while cleaning out the attic, but those are at the house, so we'll stop in there for the night tonight, and we can head out on our journey. Oh, we'll need masks and medical supplies." She was so matter-of-fact, and I couldn't help but be surprised by this. When we had finished shopping, we stopped by the cabin to grab clothes for me. I knew what I would take with me, it was always the same things: a few pairs of cargo pants, plain cotton tee shirts, a wool knit sweater, my warm jacket, acid proof rain jacket, protective gear—of which I had enough for both mother and me—underwear for a week, and the basic toiletries. Mother rented a travelling trailer which was equipped with a small kitchen, bathroom and two beds, so that we wouldn't be stuck travelling by foot, and so that we could rest rather comfortably. The trailer reminded me of trips that we would take to some of the closer Wards where we knew we would be safe. The natural surroundings always intrigued me; I was four years old when I demanded papa teach me to climb a tree, and I fell and broke my arm, once my arm had healed I climbed the tree again, and even managed to come down without so much as a sliver in my hands. Papa had been proud that I was able to do it, and mother laughed as she rustled my long brown hair. We spent that night roasting mutton, potatoes, and chestnuts on an open fire. It was an idyllic childhood memory, and my childhood was full of them.

It didn't take me long to pack all of my belongings, so we had some dinner before heading out to their house, and I decided to leave a note for Zyrene.

I'll be back in two weeks. I'm going on a trip

with my mom. Wish me luck, and eat all my food; I don't want it going bad.

Mother drove since she knew the new roads better than I did; papa was waiting for us when we arrived, he had set out some tea and sandwiches, and dziadek's notebooks for us to look through on the porch. It was a perfect June evening, the sun was low and hot, and the sky was glowing a soft pink, there was a light breeze that carried with it a moist touch, and as it hit my cheeks I closed my eyes and allowed myself a moment to escape from everything around me to imagine solitude. As the sun began to hide behind the peaks of the mountains to the West of us, papa built a fire, roasted sausages; he called all of the neighbours over, and my parents—whose government retirement fund was better than that of the incomes of those that lived in the Wards—fed the entire neighbourhood their supper that night. It wasn't until I saw just how thin some of the children were, and just how pale their skin was despite having had three good weeks of sunshine, that I began to understand why mother had argued so vehemently against the bills that were passed without the public's consent or knowledge. I had always known that my parent's position, and our life in the Centre, allowed for us to experience comfort, and safety from the elements and the unknown that lay beyond the borders of the Wards, but I never imagined that just two hours from the Centre, that I would see children so hungry, and dressed in rags. I felt ashamed for having thought that the impoverished just needed to work a little harder, that perhaps if they wrote a letter or went to see their representative that they would be provided with better, and more accessible services. I had never imagined that they didn't write letters because they simply didn't know how to write, or that their representative had his permanent residence in the Centre, and only a vacation home in the Ward. I had always been convinced that the image of prosperity that I had grown up engulfed in, was the experience of every child across the Union; it made me sick to know that I had been so ignorant of all of the suffering that went on. The Ward my parents lived in was one of the most prosperous, and so long as people could sell goods for a fair price, they would be able to survive, but in other wards they were not so lucky.

I had once heard reports of pregnant women, laying dead in the streets, or of mother's who had recently given birth coming down with infections, leaving their babies to either be nursed by a stranger, or to starve to death in the Wards farthest out from the Centre. I didn't want to believe these reports, and I had agreed with my friends when they all declared that this was made up by those who opposed the Taktikhause and its policies; but if there could be so much suffering in an area so close, and reportedly prosperous, as this, then I couldn't deny the possibility that these reports were true, perhaps somewhat exaggerated in scale, but accurate in the premise that people were suffering, and dying as we enjoyed the grandeur and esteem associated with Central living. While I had grown up with creature comforts: central heating, and air, solar powered appliances, new clothes for each season, toys piled up one on top of the other, and the best foods imaginable, those in the Wards did without new things, and passed clothes and toys down from one generation to the next, mending tears and patching holes whenever necessary. I had always known that I was well off, that my parents made a good living, and that I would never go without, but there were always little things that I pined over that were denied me. I never understood why they would send envelopes full of currency chips as gifts during WinterMas. The dirty faces, and grimy fingers of children who spent their days working to supplement their parents' income, the rail thin bodies of undernourished parents that went without so that their children could eat made it clear to me why mother worked so hard to teach me about justice. Mother looked at me and saw the anguish, and disgust in my eyes. "Now you understand why I argued so much." She got up off of her seat on the porch, and went into the house. When she had come out she was carrying a tray of sweets for the children, and they flocked to her, each one waiting patiently for theirs and thanking her for her kindness. Some even called her Baba to which she smiled and stroked their little faces. It only reminded me of the sweets that I ate liberally throughout the years, and I filled with guilt and shame.

The children ran and danced, played games and

sang songs, while their parents, despite being weary and heavy laden, laughed and shared stories of how good the winter had been for them. They asked me questions about what it was like to live in the Centre, and what it was like to have the option to go to University, to become the person that I had always wanted to be. They were genuine in their expression of joy, and surprise at my answers, and they treated me as someone who was no better, nor worse than they. "It's a matter of what you are born into." A young mother piped up from amongst the crowd. "That doesn't make it right," I called out to her "You should still have the option of making something better for yourselves, of choosing the life you want. It shouldn't matter that your children were born out in the Wards, and not in the Centre. Their birthplace doesn't make them any less intelligent or capable than children born to Central families."

"Ha!" She chortled "What do you know, honey? You've lived your life comfortably in that little fortress while the rest of us suffer out here." Her clothes were tattered, and her black hair was cut short to keep it from getting in the way of her work, her teeth were yellowed, and despite her youth her face was strewn with wrinkles.

"I don't know, I can't possibly, but that doesn't mean that I can't see the injustice for what it is. My upbringing doesn't prevent me from being a good person, but it has clouded my perception of what is happening out in the Wards. The Taktikhause has presented Central residents with an image that is false. For my entire life I have been force fed this idea that the people in the Wards are living just as well, and are finding just as much success and prosperity as we enjoyed, so it was always difficult for me, and for my friends to believe that things could be so grim out here, after all you're only an hour and a half away. Now that I've seen the hunger in your children's eyes, and the state of things out here, I know that I've been lied to. Please, let me take some footage of my own, and perhaps I can take it home with me and expose the lies." It was the only thing I could think of doing.

"Then what?" this time an old man spoke up "Wait for the Peace officers to come in and slaughter us? Don't you think we've tried? We've sent letters, made pleas with our representatives, but they don't mind our suffering! As long as we're hungry, their pantries are well stocked."

I wasn't certain what more I could say, or what else I could do to help. Whatever small gesture I made, I knew it would be met with snorts, and snuffs. I wanted to help, but it was not wanted. As the fire began to die out, and the children began to grow tired of their games, families began to file out to put the children to bed and prepare themselves for another long, hard day of work. It was difficult for me to imagine what they must have felt, knowing that even though the next day was Sunday, that it was technically required by law for them to have that day off for rest that they would work through it anyways. Sundays had always been lazy days in our house. We would sleep in until our bodies woke us, and would have a large breakfast or scrambled eggs with bacon, toast, and a bowl of fruit, then we would spend the rest of the day outdoors hiking, biking, skiing, or on particularly cold days we would sit by the fire reading, drinking hot chocolate—a rare treat that never included any real chocolate since it couldn't be grown in our climate—and we would order our dinner in from a nearby restaurant and spend the evening hours preparing ourselves for the week. Papa would sometimes try to press his own shirts, but they always ended up being scorched or over starched, so mother would playfully shove him out of the way and take over. He would then take a look at my homework, to ensure that it was in fact complete, and that I had done it correctly, I would then upload any new files necessary for the week, and help my papa prepare the week's meals. It was something that we both looked forward to, and enjoyed immensely. We wouldn't be able to spend that Sunday quite as leisurely, as we mother and I would have to examine the notebooks for any hints or directions as to uncover the lock for Dziadek's key, then we would have to pack mother's things, and finally set out on our adventure.

It was highly discouraged for Central citizens to leave the safety and comfort of the Valley, and it was not permitted for anyone who resided in the Wards to leave their Ward except by special permit—these permits were mostly reserved for workman shortages around the Centre, and in less populated Wards. Our foray beyond the borders was illegal, and we weren't certain if we would be able to get past the High Gates and fences that were built to keep the Wardsmen safe from possibly mutated wildlife. There was comfort in knowing that the Taktikhause took all necessary precautions to keep the undesired things out. There was no way for us to know their real purpose until we got to the end of the old highways where they met the gates. We hoped that the gates would be unarmed, and easy enough to open, if not then we would have to haggle our way out, or turn around and find a different route. Dziadek's journals spoke often of Lakes Eerie and Huron, so we knew that those were significant, and that there would be a place that he resided in, or would often visit, or talk about, that would contain some other morsel for us to consider in our search. I woke early on Monday morning and watched the sun rise up from the horizon, and pain the sky an array of bright colours, mother joined me on the porch with a cup of tea and fresh croissants which Papa had baked for us the night before; we spread butter and jam on our croissants, dipped them lightly in the tea and enjoyed them as they melted on our tongues into a splash of summery sweetness. Papa helped us get our things in the travel trailer, and we exchanged a long embrace. When it was mother's turn to say her farewells, they spoke for almost ten minutes, embraced, and kissed slowly, and as mother turned away, she wiped the tears from her eyes, and they let their hands slowly slide apart. They hadn't left each other's side in twenty three years.

By the time we were ready to leave it was approaching the dinner hour, so we decided it would be best to take to bed early, and head East towards where the Great Lakes had been—no one was certain if they were still there, and if they were, if they were too polluted to be considered safe. Mother's eyesight had been deteriorating slowly, so she opted to drive early in the day when she could see the road best, and then I would take the evening shift. The first hour and a half on the road was awkward; we had a hard time finding things to talk about, and I wasn't entirely certain what kinds of things I could tell my mother, and what kinds of stories she had saved to tell me in person. When we arrived at the first Ward boundary, we presented our chips for scanning. "Where are you heading?" The female officer asked us, the brown uniform did little to highlight the fact that she was a woman. "Just taking a tour of the Wards ma'am; after all, my mother is the great Danuta Weitzman, and she helped build this." She stepped back, tipped her hat, and waved us through. We couldn't help but laugh as soon as we were out of earshot; it was the first time since I was little that I had heard mother laugh so full heartedly. "Ahhh," she sighed and wiped a tear away, the lines around her eyes were visible as she smiled "I can't believe that you pulled the name card! Well done, darling, well done. You know, when I was younger I would never have bothered with it, I would have just spoken circles around her, making up some story or another about how I had important research to conduct, and that the paperwork had not yet come through. I would have turned it all around and blamed it on her incompetence, but I was much crueler than you." Her smile faded, and there in front of me sat a woman that I had never truly known, and one whom I wished desperately to understand completely.

We drove in a comfortable silence for two hours; we had each brought some of our favourite music with us on outdated mp3 tech—mother had made a point to get a trailer that allowed for us to be comfortable, but untracked—and we had finally come across an old lyric*:*

He said, Try to go on
Take my books, take my gun
Remember, my son, how they lied
And the night comes on
It's very calm
I'd like to pretend that my father was wrong
But you don't want to lie, not to the young

Cohen's haunting words rang in our ears, and lingered in the air, and I began my journey to understanding mother's ruthlessness in truth. Mother had never lied to me; at least not about the important things, the things that would shape my politics, my values, and ultimately my adult life. I had resented her for being too honest when I was a child. She would often answer my questions about the Wards with a brief statement on the rights and wrongs of the Taktikhause's approach on keeping the Wards in line. I had a difficult time understanding it as a child; I suppose any child would, but it was her responsibility to teach me what the State run schools wouldn't. She made it a point to make me understand my privilege, and to hate it, to hate that I had been born into a corrupt system— and particularly a system that could have been created to be equal, to be fair. Papa always believed that, as with animal packs, certain people were just bound to be Alphas, that they were strong, charismatic, and charming, and so through their use of Wit, and social graces, they would find a way to make things work for their own benefit, and not for the benefit of the Betas. He called it "a dog eat dog world", and mother hated it. She had always been a communist at heart, and had always believed that all resources should be shared equally, and that all people who are able should contribute equally. Papa thought it foolish to assume that a population of five million could possibly function this way, I was inclined to agree with him, but now that

I had seen the injustice first hand, I couldn't help but wonder if there could be a healthy compromise. Perhaps that was what this adventure would reveal. Mother sat with her eyes closed, her features were relaxed, the sun beamed down upon her face and gave her a spectacular glow; and her chest rose rapidly each time she inhaled as she hummed along. She had never looked so beautiful.

TRADITIONS

We continued to follow the Hope Highway; it was the only highway that would lead us straight through the last Ward, and open up to the unknown world beyond. We stopped in a small, rundown shanty town to stretch our legs, and—as was part of mother's intentions for our adventure—support the local community. The children were better fed, and many of them had newer looking clothes, which was unsurprising considering the local industry was farming, and even though it was punishable by death to grow food for personal use—as a means of discouraging rivalries between families, encouraging equality, and keeping the peace in the outlying Wards—most families in the farming Wards kept a small personal garden, or community garden to help stave off hunger during the long winter months; some even ventured to travel to other communities and trade bushel for bushel for cotton, berries, grains, and even meats. One older woman who ran a pastry shop regaled us with tales of how families would come together to build store houses, or to assist a new mother with caring for her baby and family, and how it was their custom to always have an extra place set at the table for those who were less fortunate. Her lips were full and moist, and her skin looked soft and supple though it was well weathered and wrinkled with flour and baking powder caught in the creases. She smelled of shortbread and jam, and the pastry shop was expertly lined with colourful petite fours. "We've saved many a starvin' babe and their mommas just by simply letting them in our doors to rest, 'n' fill their bellies. Miss Bellie, she runs the sewin' shop 'cross the way; now that child was but twelve years ol' when she and her momma came rappin' at my door. Such a sweet lookin' girl she was, but rail thin, and the poor dear had no colour left in her. Now she's all grown and strong, and set to marry my boy! That was the deal we made with her momma, my boy took such a shinin' to her from the moment he saw her, so he says to me, he say 'Momma, we'll help that child and her momma, but only if she promises to marry me!' I looked at that girl, and thought, such a pretty thing would give me some nice lookin' grandbabies and the such. They been coupled ever since! We fed that child, gave her a warm place to rest her head, taught her how to read and even to write some, and just enough arithmetic to run the shop. Her momma left the poor thang with us, and went on elsewhere." Mother called it a Texan accent, the way that her vowels lingered, and she cut the words off just as they were about to end, the way she almost sang through a sentence made me feel secure, even though her story was horrifying.

"How old was your son?" Mother's tone was careful, non-judgemental despite the fact that I could see in her eyes how disgusted she was at the idea of selling your child.

"He was nineteen when she first came to us, and that was some ten years ago; twenty-one's the legal marryin' age 'round these parts, though kids go to their kinfolk and get hitched at 'round the age of sixteen, then their folk build 'em a nice house to start raisin' up some babies. There ain't no proper school out here, so we teach 'em ourselves." We thanked her for her kindness and hospitality, and left as quickly as possible. Mother kept silent until we got to the trailer, but her breathing was rapid, and uneven.

"Can you believe the gall of that woman?!? She ought to know better; I mean, I could understand if someone who had been born after the...but this, this woman, she's old enough to know!" Her face turned red, and tears welled up in her eyes; I saw her guilt, she knew she was responsible for the state of this girl's life. She got out of the trailer, and walked quickly, her arms swinging wildly, towards the sewing store; I ran after my mother, in hopes to either stop her, or save her if something in our unspoken plan went awry. She shoved the door to the shop open, "Miss Bellie?" she called out in an authoritative tone "Miss Bellie, I need to speak with you!" Her tone softened. The shutter door flew open, and the twenty-one year old girl stepped through;

she was tall, and her legs were long, her dress was long, and looked like something I'd seen in my "History of Art" text about the seventeenth Century, her features were soft, and reminded me of a painting of an Indian Princess. "Yes?" Her voice was soft, and pleasant. "Are you Miss Bellie?" Mother asked "Yes, I am." She spoke with less of an accent than the bake shop woman, and her words were clear "May I help you?"

"No," mother began "but we are going to help you!" she wasn't willing to leave without this girl.

"Excuse me?" Miss Bellie's brow furrowed in confusion.

"You are coming with us; I'm Dani Weitzman, and this is my daughter Marie. Do you know who I am?" Mother wasn't very tactful.

"Yes, I know who you are. Why would I go with you?" her confusion was compounding, and she looked ready to tip over in her oversized dress, and corset.

"You do not have to marry that man! That, that poor excuse for a woman across the street told us about how your mother—who probably felt she had no other choice—left you with her on the condition that you would marry her son. You do not owe that family a single thing! Now, take only what you need, and you are coming with us!" Mother was short with the poor girl, who could hardly make out what mother was saying, let alone figure out what was about to happen.

"Mom!" I took mother by the shoulders and looked at the shocked girl "Look," I took her small, soft hands in my large rough ones "your mother-in-law explained the custom here, about how you were promised to her son, and so forth. We are giving you an opportunity to leave here, to never, ever be forced to get married again. You're a woman, not an object!" I made my voice soft, gentle, and compassionate. I could see in her that she had never allowed herself to consider the possibility of leaving, of escaping a fate that she assumed was unavoidable. She was beside herself, and paced frantically trying to work through the possibilities "But, what could I do? Where could I go? We're not allowed to leave the Ward. The laws say so. I would be a fugitive, and no one would help me. This is just the way it is, and I just have to accept that." Her voice was low for a woman's, and it had a grizzly quality to it. She knew that her reality was grim, and that no matter how hard she tried that she would never escape it. "You'll come with us." The words escaped my mouth before I could even consider the logistics of how to smuggle this woman out "We have enough food, clothes, water, and space to take you with us. You'll be safe, and we'll find a way to keep you from this fate. I promise!"

"Listen," she placed her hands on her hips "I ain't no fool, and I know the law just as well as anyone 'round here. So, don't you go tellin' me that you'll find a way, and makin' promises that there ain't no way for y'all to keep. It's downright ridiculous! Now, unless y'all are plannin' on buyin' something you'll excuse me; I've got some mendin' to do." Her intonation changed, the way she rolled her words melted into the local accent, and her expression become one of frustration and upset. It was then that both mother and I realized that there was little we could do to help change these kinds of customs, and the women bound to them; and that the further away from the Centre that we got, the stranger, and more barbaric these customs would become. We got back into the trailer, and mother's eyes filled with rage "It's my fault; Parliament Hill, the contracts, all of it." I had never seen her so broken. "If only I hadn't made those tapes, or if I had reported something to the RCMP or to CSIS. Everything could have been different. You know?" She had always masked her guilt with anger towards the Taktikhause, except out here, these nuances, this trade of women, was beyond what the Taktikhause could legislate. "It could've been worse, mom" I had never been very good at comforting others, "I mean, who knows what would have happened if you hadn't exposed the plot." I wasn't sure where to go from there, what more could I say; maybe things would have been better, maybe there would be more people still living, maybe, just maybe the whole point was to tip the scales. We would never know, so what was the point of coming up with all of those "maybes"? "Mom, look," I took a deep breath in, not certain how she would react "there is no point in getting pissed off at yourself; seriously, yes this shit out here is weird, and yes people out here are suffering, but wasn't it like that before? Except instead, it was entire countries; millions, billions of children starving to death! At least we can help fix this, or at the very least keep it from getting worse. It just won't freakin' help to sit here and mope about what could have been." My hands shook, and my cheeks burned, I was afraid of what she would say, or perhaps I was afraid that she would think I was right. Mother had once had a fighting spirit, but in recent years, as more and more problems became known to her, and as the Taktikhause garnered more power, and took liberties away from the people it was supposed to represent under the guise of security and prosperity, she had become defeated. My gaze was fixed on her, I waited for what felt like hours for her to say something, or worse get out of the trailer and do something drastic. She just sat there and breathed deeply, with control, her foot taping rapidly, she had her eyes closed and her back was straight and tall—she had always chided me for slumping whenever I sat down. Her eyes shot open, and the sunlight made them a ghostly grey, she took a final deep breath in. "Well, what are you sitting there for, start her up, and lets go figure this key out. Maybe dziadek left some sort of guide for us to use, or at least some kind of advice." We pushed onward for the rest of the day, and as we drove through small towns, and farms we had all we could do to not pull over and hand out food to every sickly child we passed. The numbers grew larger as we drove further out, and soon all we could find was emaciated bodies; people who were too hungry, too sick, too tired, to get off of the side of the road, presumably on their way to find food, shelter, clean water. We would see families gathered around the tiny body of a small child, whose body was nothing more than skin and bone, crying out to a deity that would never hear them.

INTERRUPTIONS

Religion had been outlawed from the Centre since the very beginning; churches, mosques, synagogues, all places of worship were kept only as historical sites, and above ground emergency shelters; we had learned about different religions in school, and mother had tried to share with me her understanding of faith, and how a benevolent god could allow humanity to suffer. I had never understood it, but I suppose it could be a comfort to those who would never know the feeling of a full belly, or health. Mother and I stopped to stretch our legs, and we stood, horrified, as peace officers—dressed all in black, with surgical masks and gloves—carried the bodies of an entire family out, and set fire to the house that they had occupied; the only survivor was a two week old infant. Mother ran to the officers "Please, stop, stop!" she knew that in situations like this the child would be administered a series of injections, because the only other option was to let him starve. I had never seen mother run so fast "Please! I will take him! I will take responsibility for him!" I ran after her. The officer who held the baby stopped, and the others looked to him. "He will have to be scanned for disease first, and then we can consider adoption, but you're a little old aren't you lady?" His voice was deep and captivating; it was the kind of voice that I could see myself listening to endlessly. "Excuse me, sir," I stepped forward, my breathing rapid after running after mother "My mother and I will take responsibility for the child. Here, look" I rolled up my sleeve, and extended my arm to him so that he could scan my identifier "My name is Marie Weitzman, and this is my mother Danuta Weitzman. You ought to know who she is." He removed his helmet, passed the infant to his inferior officer, and removed his mask. He had a strong, square jaw, and his green eyes were bright against his dark skin, his lips were full and soft—the kind that I would have enjoyed kissing—he smiled widely, and approached us with his scanner. "Well, it's a true honour ma'am. I'm sorry if I offended you in any way. I'm Sergeant Joseph Conroy, and these are my men." His grip was firm, but gentle, and he stood close to me as he watched for my identification and authorizations to come up on his screen; he smelled of leather and the muskiness of firewood. "Now," he took mother's arm "there are procedures that we have to follow. I'm sure that you ladies are in a bit of a hurry to tour the Wards, after all" he turned his gaze towards me, and I felt jittery "you need to be back in the Centre in only ten days to begin your duties as a Conservateur, but we really do have to go through the proper channels." His expression darkened, and sorrow filled his eyes "We have to make sure that the baby didn't catch any illnesses from its mother, and if it did we have to," he licked his lips and took in a deep breath "contain the infection. I'll send my men on towards the Illness Recovery Centre, and I'll give you two a tour of the area, perhaps you would like to better understand what we're up against out here." He walked around to my side, and placed his hand gently on the centre of my back. He was a relatively tall man, his shoulders broad, and well muscled. He would have been intimidating to the citizens at first glance, but I could see that he was well liked by children in the area; he even carried a bag of fruit and seeds to share with them. Mother had opted to continue on with the other officers, so that she could keep a close watch on the baby.

We spent the remainder of the afternoon walking around, talking about the needs of the Wardsmen; after a couple of hours of walking in the July sun we sat down on a rock near the creek and he shared his fear that most of the children would not survive to their twelfth birthdays, and his eyes swelled with tears. I couldn't help but wipe them away with my thumb— the men back home were too proud to cry in front of women, especially women whom they didn't know. "Well, we should probably go and check on that baby, and see how your mother is handling the IRC." He stood up, and then helped pull me up. My foot slipped on the slimy pebbles underneath our feet, and we both fell into the water. I was mortified, and I could feel the blood rushing to my face as I blushed. "Are you alright?" he called after me. "Oh, just bruised my pride is all. I swear I'm normally much better coordinated." He had swum to me, and was wrapping his arms around my waist, and the warmth of his body against my back was almost too much. We reached shallow waters, and walked the rest of the way to shore, I had worn my pink silk blouse, and denim Capri's, and they clung to me, exposing every curvature of my body as we slowly emerged from the water; the current was rapid and strong, and had pulled us some twenty feet downstream. The sergeant continued to hold onto my waist, and it was a good thing that he did, or else I would have continued to float away. The rocks under our feet were slimy, and my sandals had floated off down the river. "I could carry you if you'd like." His offer was genuine, but I couldn't allow myself to be even more indebted to him. "Please, allow me, at least until we get back to the roads; you're going to get something stuck in your foot, and then you'll be contained in the IRC."

"Fine." I rolled my eyes and crossed my arms in front of my breasts in a sad attempt at modesty. "Can we please stop in at my trailer first? I need to change, and we can quickly dry your things as well."

"Are you sure?" His Adam's apple rose and fell as he swallowed hard, and subtly, almost subconsciously bit his lip "I mean about my things, I don't want to put you out." The forest floor was soft under my feet, and I would have spent the entire evening just strolling through, finding interesting plants and insects, trying to understand the impact radiation had had on the wilderness. "Oh, it's no problem at all. It should only take fifteen minutes or so to dry them." I let my hips sway as I began to walk a little ahead. When he caught up, he crouched down so that I could climb onto his back. My clothes clung to me, and my body struggled against them to wrap its arms and legs around him. As we passed some of the villagers, skulking to their homes, their clothes hanging off of their frail bodies, I caught their glimpses, and unapproving sneers.

When we got in, he took his clothes off as I stood with my back turned to him, facing the window watching hollow bodied men slouch with heavy bags towards the industrial centre. He sat at the small table wrapped in a towel as I placed his things in the dryer and snuck into the bathroom to change. I peeled my blouse and capris off, and as I turned away from the mirror to grab my dry clothes from the hook, I noticed the red bumps on my back, and neck, and on the backs of my arms. "Oh, shit!" I came out of the bathroom in my pink lace bra and matching panties, he looked at me and I could see he was confused "Look at my back! What is that?" I was panicked. He stood up carefully, and looked at me, studied my skin. "Hmmm, looks like an allergic reaction, but we should take you to get evaluated just in case." He stood there thinking for a moment. "Hold on, I've got some gloves in my pack." He pulled up a stool, snapped the gloves on, and ran his hands, gently, down my neck and back, and across my arms, he took swabs of my skin, "Do you have any tea?" "What?" I turned around, my breasts were perfectly in line with his face, and he couldn't help but chortle. "Oh God! This really is not how I want any man to see me half naked for the first time." I buried my face in my hands. He stood up "Trust me, it could be worse." He walked to the kitchen counter "Tea can help soothe the spots, I really don't think it's illness related; the onset is too quick. It could just be that there's something on our forest floor, or in the algae on the rocks that you're allergic to."

"Oh." I grabbed the tea out of the cupboard and put on the water to boil. "What do you mean by 'it could be worse'?"

"Well," he stepped closer "You could be completely naked, but that would seem better to me." My heat began to race, and my face flushed. The kettle whistled. He poured the water over the tea bag. "Now, we just have to wait for it to cool." He pulled away and went back to the table where he shuffled a deck of cards. I put the tea in the refrigerator, grabbed my favourite oversized shirt, and threw it on. "What are we playing?" I sat down across from him. "Gin-Rummy; nice shirt." He smirked "I don't know why you put it on; you'll just have to take it off in a bit anyways." He was smug.

"Why don't you put your uniform back on, it

should be dry by now." It was the only retort I could think of at the time, but he was comfortable, and enjoyed the playfulness of it. We played one hand then grabbed the chilled tea; by that time I was terribly itchy, and the shirt felt like someone had put me in a burlap sack. "Alright, Sergeant, please get this shirt off of me!" the pain was written all over my face. He was gentle, and made sure that his hands didn't touch my skin as he slipped the shirt off.. I could feel his eyes scanning me, assessing the amount of damage, and how urgently I might need medical attention that he was not qualified to give. He gently sponged my entire body with the tea; with each stroke I was flooded with relief, and he read it in my face. "You know, you don't have to call me Sergeant, just call me Joey."

"Alright, Joey. You don't look, or sound like you grew up out here. So, what's your story?" My voice was strained from the pain. "Well," his voice was comforting, and I needed to get lost in it "I was born in what used to be Montana, and when I was only six weeks old, momma packed me and my sisters up and went on foot in the dead of winter to the Centre. She had heard about it from friends of hers that were planning on making the trip, so we all went together. We were permitted entrance, but since we had nothing to offer as far as goods are concerned we were assigned to the Wards. My momma was given a small stipend to help with the first two years, so we settled out in the farming ward. It was good for some time, but as my sisters got to be twelve, thirteen years old, families started approaching us and offering her large sums of crop yields for them. Some of the wealthy families were experiencing problems with infertility, so they wanted to buy themselves a handmaid or two. My mother refused to sell them, so they burnt down our farm. We sought help from the local peace officers, but they didn't want to get involved in local customs and family feuds." He paused, "Your back is done, turn around." He waited quietly for me to turn "Anyways," he rung the cloth with me standing between his legs, his eyes scanning and assessing my body, "momma decided we needed to go elsewhere, maybe find a place where selling girls to be sex slaves wasn't normal. I was six years old, and had heard and seen too much already."

His hands worked gently and quickly, and never lingered where their touch might not be wanted. "That's when I decided I wanted to do something to change the lives of children in the Wards; to do something good. Since she had decided to settle in the farming ward, we could only move further out to a different town. Things were a little better there, and girls weren't traded, the only thing that was strange to us was that marriages were pre-arranged. The town's mayor said that it was to ensure that the children would be able to have a happy and normal life as they grew up, and that it would safeguard future generations from poverty and starvation. She agreed to do it, but only if the girls could be part of the decision. We got to know the boys at school, and momma made it a point to host block parties so that she could figure out which families would be best suited to blend with our family. In the end, the girls chose men who would turn out to be good to them, and who were very good at farming. My eldest sister has five kids now, and they are all doing very well, and they use their surplus to help the poorer families, and my other sister is a widow. Her husband died a few years ago from radiation sickness—he drank from a contaminated well while he was out surveying an unpopulated area some fifty kilometers from their home. And me, well I was sent here right out of the academy." He had stopped sponging me down half way through, and was staring down at the floor. I took his chin by my right hand and pulled him towards me. The towel that was wrapped around his waist fell to the ground as he pulled me into his warmth. "Stay with me?" He whispered it in my ear, and it sounded like more of a promise than a question as he kissed me.

When we arrived at the IRC, mother was pacing in the front lobby. "There you are!" She looked at me curiously, then at Joey. "Oh, well, good for you two! It's about time Marie stopped being so level headed."

"Mom!" I was shocked, and I looked to Joey to step in and make some excuse or another, but he just smiled, and pulled me in.

"Oh please, I was twenty-one once too! I recognize that look of guilt and joy just as well as I felt it when Papa and I...well you know." Her mind traveled back to when they were first together, to the day that everything changed. "Anyways, never mind that. They won't tell me a single thing about the baby" her gaze moved from the long hallway in front of her back towards Joey "is there anything that you can do, Sergeant?"

"It's Joey, ma'am, and I think I might be able to find something out." He let go of me as we turned the corner, and his face hardened into that of the Peace Officer that he had been trained to be. It was then that I knew I could love him, that I could be with him and never get tired; mother saw it in the way a small smile crept across my face, and my eyes lit up. "Lucky boy, that one." She nudged me with her elbow. "Oh, mother please!" I rolled my eyes at her—it was my only defence against her intuition. We stayed back behind the cold steel doors, waiting for a report back. The waiting made me think about my rash, and it began to itch and burn against the heat of my cotton shirt. "What are you scratching for child?" Mother shot me a look just as she had when I had come down with chickenpox as a little girl. "Oh, I slipped into the river and my sandals floated downstream; I think I must have stepped on something and broke out in hives. Joey managed to fish me out, and ended up carrying me through the streets back to the trailer. Maybe we can find an apothecary shop, or a doctor that can prescribe something for the rash?"

"Maybe, but you may want to stop scratching before you start bleeding, or before you draw too much attention towards it, and get put under containment." She had taken hold of my hands to still them. "So, tell me, darling, what did you learn about that handsome young man?"

"Seriously? You want to have that talk now? Here?" She never ceased to amaze me.

"Let's call it taking your mind off of this itch." She sat me down on a cold hard plastic chair with chrome legs next to coffee-flavoured drink machine, and held my hands still. She watched me thoughtfully as I told her what little I knew about him; about how he felt, and how he smelled, how his hands were careful yet demanding. It felt more like talking with Zyrene rather than talking to my mother. "He sounds wonderful!" there was happiness in her eyes.

"Sorry that that took so long," Joey pulled off

the mask and gloves "They have finished taking samples, he has had a complete physical exam and scans. He looks to be in good health, no parasites, no broken or missing limbs, ten fingers, ten toes, a healthy looking and active brain. We just need to wait for the pathology reports to come back. The doctor is pretty certain that he will pass, and that you will be able to take him with you." His eyes darted to me, begging me not to leave. Mother excused herself. "I can't stay right now." I knew it wasn't what he wanted to hear, but what I had to tell him "I have to finish this tour with my mother. We're looking for something that my grandfather left hidden somewhere, and it's important to her that we find it. When we're done with that, I'll go home and perhaps you could request a transfer, and I could sponsor you. We could see where things go from there." I saw that he was hurt.

"You don't understand, do you?" He looked at me compassionately "When you signed the papers to begin the process of assuming guardianship over baby Zairinth, you agreed to stay here as long as was necessary for the process to be completed. The Science

Institute has been informed, and you're being temporarily transferred here, until the baby can be said to travel safely. You'll have to postpone your trip, or your mother will, but one of you has to stay here." I stood up. I was angry that he neglected to tell me this before, my eyes scanned him. "I'm sorry Marie. I thought you knew that that is how this process works. The exception is if the child is being adopted from beyond the Ward's boundary, only then can the adoptive parents remain away from the child." His voice was gentle as he placed his hands on my arms.

How had I not known this, I had read the papers, I had studied adoption processes in a Social Justice course that I had taken; I couldn't justify being angry at him. I had forgotten this amendment because I had always assumed it would never affect me. How had I allowed myself to get so wrapped up in the moment to forget that saving this one child would mean sacrificing at least three months stuck in an isolated Ward? Mother would have called it a new chapter on our adventure together, but I was not like her, at least not in this aspect. I took in a cleansing breath, and decided that I would simply just have to accept this new reality, this temporary home.

Mother and I sent a telegram to Papa about the little fork in our road, and I sent one to Zyrene to let her know that she could sub-let on a month to month basis while I was away. I simply told her that I had received a last minute transfer. Being single made it a likely story. Joey took the next week off and we spent it looking for a place where mother and I could set up a temporary home, taking shifts with mother at the IRC to check on the baby, and sneaking in some time away from everything, and everyone. That Wednesday we decided to go back out the river, my rash had cleared up with the help of some herbal ointment from the local apothecary, and it was a dead hot summer day. My equipment would arrive in a week's time, and my only job until then was to get accustomed to the surroundings. Joey helped me to study the maps that I had been sent to my electroslate; he helped me identify landmarks, and areas that were known for strange occurrences. He begged me to avoid them, or at least not to go there without him. I accepted his offer. We had brought lunch with us, and enjoyed the feeling of the hot sun bouncing off of the mist that rose from the river and peppered our faces with dew as we ate and laughed. My life of privilege seemed foolish, and the things that I had perceived as being problematic as a child, were of completely no significance to what he had faced, but none-the-less he listened to me with compassion and caring. I was amazed that a man who had seen his mother have to hand over the last of what she had left of her husband—a platinum watch—to keep the landlord from kicking them out onto the street, who could do nothing but stand idly by as his childhood girlfriends were married off or sold for their own protection, but then would walk past him in the market with bruises, burns, and scars and pregnant bellies, that even he could understand how my minor inconveniences could seem devastating to me. He had witnessed injustice on a daily basis, and felt powerless to change it, and I had lived a life of luxury and complained over any minor disturbance in that comfort. I felt immense guilt over my stories of woe, but he wouldn't have it. "It's what you knew." His eyes were fixated on mine "how can you feel badly because you were unaware of the injustices as a child? How could you even have known they existed when this is the first you've seen of them? None of your friends back in the Centre will understand, and most of them will never see it." His gentleness was overwhelming, and I couldn't talk any longer. "Take me to your place. I haven't seen it yet." I stood up, more carefully this time, and stretched out my hand to him. He hopped off of the rock, took my hand and led me back to his car.

His house was on the outskirts of the town, it was amid a row of truly lovely houses, there was green grass in the front, and flower boxes that lined the front of the house; the door was a bright red, like strawberries in early August, and the siding was a pale cream. The windows were trimmed in a chocolate brown, and the awning was made of cedar slabs. It was a spacious two-story home, which seemed excessive for a man who lived alone. "So, why the big house?" I turned to face him as he shut the door behind us. "Well, this is the one that they gave me upon transfer out here. The rooms are rarely empty, and I've even built

Additional rooms in the basement. I usually let families with small children stay here so that they can have a safe place to sleep, and a decent amount of food in their bellies. Some of my colleagues have started to do the same. It's the best way that we can help. Come, I'll show you around." The idea was inspiring.

    He had five large rooms on the upper level, and each one was fitted with a queen sized bed, a crib, and an Additional queen sized fold-away bed; each room had easy access to the bathroom, and there was a schedule pinned up with times for showers and baths for each room, so that there wouldn't be any problems. In the basement he had built four more rooms like the ones upstairs. On the main floor was a large open kitchen with maple cabinets, and granite counters, he had a large oak table that could easily seat twenty adults in the dining room; there was also the living room with a working wood burning fireplace, an area for children to play and learn, a library full of paper books that smelled heavenly, and finally his bedroom which was small in comparison to the others and housed a single sized bed on a simple frame, a small night table with a lamp, alarm clock, and lock box for his sidearm, and a small wardrobe. I sat him down on the bed, and began to undress. He wrapped his arms around me, and pulled me down on top of him. I would have loved to spend the rest of the day in his arms, but we only had an hour before Mother would be expecting us at the IRC, and it would take us fourty five minutes to drive down.

The doctor was waiting for us with the results of all of the scans, and mother paced around the waiting room; as we stepped in the through the door, she stopped. "Well," Dr. Eagleman gestured to us to sit "All of the scans are complete, and I've spent most of the afternoon analyzing their results." He took a sip of his hot caffeine drink, and swallowed loudly. "Now, overall the child is without infections, and has no signs of genetic anomalies present." We let go of a sigh of relief. Our time here would be brief, and it would only be a couple of months before we could return to the Centre. "But, there is the matter of his neurological development."

"What do you mean?" Mother had risen from

her seat, her hands were placed firmly on her hips, and her brow was furrowed.

"Please, stay calm. There is nothing necessarily wrong with the child, and there are definitely no code alterations, or function disturbances, but there is some neuro-developmental delay. His reflexes aren't particularly strong, and it's possible that his mother's breast milk wasn't nourishing enough—it's quite common out here. Most women will forego meals so that their husbands and children can eat, but what they don't realize is that it directly affects the quality of their breast milk." He took another sip of his beverage. "Now, that isn't to say that with a medically supervised diet from here-on-in that he can't catch up to other children his age. The other problem though, is if he doesn't improve with a nutrient rich diet." His eyes grew closer together, and there was genuine concern and regret in his expression. "What is it doc?" Joey knew that whatever the doctor had to say, that I would be devastated, and that mother would be angry. "Well, if he doesn't improve, there are two options: he will either have to be placed under supervision with a specialized program to assist him in learning to perform basic tasks, or if his guardians choose to surrender him to the Authority of Taktikhause, he will be euthanized."

"Those don't sound like options." I was bewildered, and the idea of letting him suffer was unconscionable, and the thought of surrendering him to his death was sickening. "In either case, will he ever be able to function normally? You know, go to school, have a first kiss, a first dance, a good job, wife, kids?" I wanted to give him everything that I was given, and I had often dreamt of what he would be when he reached adulthood. My heart sank, I had grown to love this child, and I looked at him as if I had given him life.

"I know it seems bleak, but we have hope for a full recovery here. You were the ones who begged for us to spare him; if not for you, he would have been injected almost immediately." There was no denying that this man had the displeasure of putting down many orphaned infants in his time there, and the sorrow and self-disgust festered in his eyes. "Please," he choked on his tears 'please, help me save at least this one. I've had so many others that have had to be" he paused, searching for the gentlest way to say murdered "given back to God that I've lost count. Please, just this one!" It never occurred to me to let my boy be killed for no other reason than having been born to a family struggling to survive. I took his hand in mine, and gently squeezed in an attempt to show what I could not bring myself to say. We signed the last of the papers in his room. The final page allowed us to rename him, but his name, his heritage, his whole life could not be erased from my mind, and so we named him: Adalhard Zairinth Weitzman. His skin had gained colour, and had a beautiful bronze glow, and his eyes were clear and an engrossing green. We wrapped him in a blanket that mother had spent her watches knitting, and carried him to Joey's house. We would have to keep a home in Maragujju for a minimum of six months, so we reorganized some of the rooms in his house to make space for mother, myself and Addie

GAINING GROUND

Addie progressed well once the doctor had found a synthetic milk that had the right levels of nutrients for him, and the fear that he would be unable to function well began to subside. We had put two months of work into taking care of our boy, and focusing only on his needs, and we had almost completely forgotten about the key. I spent an afternoon—it was a beautiful mid-fall day, and the air was crisp with the smell of death—preparing for the fall festival, and as I moved our summer clothing into boxes, the key fell out of my Capri pants onto the hard wooden floor. When it hit the ground the sound of its weight was thick, and brought to mind the importance of discovering dziadek's secrets, to finding the solution for the injustice that Addie was born into; the disparity that could have killed him. I flipped the key through my fingers, as my mind wandered through its own version of the adventure that we had to continue on.

At supper that evening with the air still in the house, and the steam of hot stew rising from the bowls into our faces, and the soft sounds of Addie's breath as he slept in his cradle I pulled they key out from the pocket of my cardigan, and slid it towards mother. She smiled in her mischievous way, and I knew that she hadn't forgotten, she had simply been waiting for me to be ready. "We'll pack up after Fall festival, and head to Lake Eerie. It was his favourite one, and he mentioned a lake house in his journals several times. He was only redundant when he needed to point out something's importance." She didn't look up from her dinner, she was so composed, so calm, as though we had always had Addie with us. "But, mom, what about the baby? Risking our own lives, our own exposure to radiation is one thing, but we can't endanger him like that." I had forgotten about the trailer, that it had been lined with Reluctorad. All mother had to do to jog my memory was give me a disapproving look—she wasn't one to take uncalculated risks, at least not since Parliament Hill.

I had spent my days in the surrounding meadows, taking samples, readings, and plotting charts, and my evenings giving every ounce of love I could muster to Addie and Joey. Joey's work had become more difficult as more of those living in the outlying areas got sick, and he was forced to bring entire neighbourhoods of people to the IRC for study. Some began to whisper that these people were being brought there to be infected, that the Taktikhause wanted to get rid of those who were looked upon as a scourge—the poor, the underprivileged. He was becoming disheartened, and the bright light in his eyes faded into a slight twinkling, which only lit as he held Addie. "You're coming with us." I crawled under the blanket, and put my cold feet in between his warm ones. "God, you're freezing!" He pulled his feet away, but I was persistent, and this was our game. "I have a job to do here; I can't leave now, not when things are getting bad." I hadn't seen him smile in over a week, and his heart was heavy with the burden of knowing that sixty percent of those that he would take to the IRC wouldn't come out, and that forty percent of those would be children and infants. "That's precisely why you have to come with us!" I turned his face towards mine "I've heard some whispers, Joe. They're not happy out there, and they want to force things to change. These people are sick and hungry, and they won't stop until they're either all dead or have what they want." The thought of him dying at the hands of an angry mob, or because some sick beggar coughed on him was overwhelming in its probability. "I need you to come with us." It was the closest that I could get to pleading with him. "I don't know." It was the closest he would ever come to a promise.

Mother and I packed up all of our clothes, and all of Addie's things; we needed to return within a month for his check in with the IRC staff, so that they could note his progress, but I had this sneaking suspicion that we wouldn't return to see them. We climbed into the trailer leaving Joey behind, he had been called in to take over a patrol. As we drove beyond the Eastern gate of the town, we heard the earth shattering bang of homemade explosives going off, mother was driving, and pushed down hard on the accelerator, I jumped to the back to check on Addie in his safety seat; he was terrified, and his crying was shrill. Our ears were thudding, and there was a small trickle of blood coming from his left ear; I could only hope that the damage wouldn't be permanent. I peeked out the back window of the trailer and saw the ridge of upper class housing on fire; the black smoke rose and blanketed the sky—we had left just in time—and the screams and shouts of hundreds of burning bodies could be heard for miles. We had only a day's worth of driving ahead of us before we would reach the Gate, and we weren't certain what to expect when we got there.

There were rumours that the Gate was completely sealed to keep residents inside, as if in some vast prison, and other rumours touted that the Gate was a myth, that it was simply a fence designed to keep strange, mutated wildlife out. Others still claimed that the gate was protected by droids that were designed to keep things in and out. There were many rumours that floated around, and each individual had his or her own take on it; even children would tell the stories differently from their own parents. We stopped every two hours to check on Addie, we tested his hearing, fed him, changed him, played with him, and when he had sufficiently stretched his legs we buckled him into his safety seat and kept driving, but never did we leave him sitting in the back alone. I could sit with him and watch as he slept for hours on end, but mother had me keeping an eye on the maps, and updated me constantly as to our location. She was adamant that we stay our course.

We arrived at Burderton by late evening, and we decided to stop just outside of town—far enough so that we wouldn't be found unawares, but close enough so that we could make good time the next morning. Papa had made certain to install motion and heat sensitive surveillance cameras so that we could be constantly aware if someone approached the trailer. We had a restful night. The pink of the sky permeated the shutters, and the trailer was flooded in a sea of colour as the sun rose, mother woke early, and took a brisk walk—she had always believed in being physically fit, and the time spent behind the wheel was giving her aches and pains that she had never had before. When she returned I had already prepared our breakfast. We decided to drive into town, and take Addie for a walk, allow him some time in the sun, and fresh air. When we stepped out, the cold air nipped at our noses, our breath froze, and my skin felt tight; mother smiled. She drew in a deep breath. "Ahhhhhh" there was contentment in her expression "This is what winter felt like when I was little. There were days, before the gray snow started to fall, that dziadek would send me out to play and as I stepped out the door I could feel the frost form on my cheeks, and in my hair. That's how I knew that I would be able to go fast on my sled, and that building a snowman, or making a snow fort would be difficult, but it was a challenge that I welcomed." I had never known a winter that cold; since the Final War, the winters had been rather warm—the temperature rarely went any lower than minus ten degrees Celsius—so it was shocking to me that this place could be so much colder than the Centre despite its altitude. Or perhaps, something had changed, perhaps the Centre was experiencing record lows. The thought of Zyrene scrambling to find clothes that could possibly keep her warm enough to get to and from work without arriving the colour of sapphires, was enough to make me laugh loudly. When I explained it to mother, she chortled. We didn't walk for long, but the cold air worked wonders on our spirits, and seemed to brighten Addie as well. It was my turn to drive, so mother sat in the back with him, and told him old tales, fairy stories, recited plays, and sang nursery rhymes, and the whole time Addie stared at her, gurgling away, spitting out the occasional babbling sound. His hearing in his left ear didn't appear to be damaged, and he seemed to enjoy mother's stories. The drive was scenic, the rise and fall of the landscape engulfed in a light blue frost, with the heavy hand of fog sprawling across the hills, and the bare Oak branches juxtaposed with the tall, firm Pines still dark in their never ending green, rose up and reached out to grab hold of what little warmth the geese could provide as they stopped to rest during their migration. It was breathtaking. Mother sat at the window with Addie, and pointed out trees, and ruined houses, and the fifteen foot tall fence that appeared on the horizon, beyond the fog, and the hills. We were only a few hours away from the Gate, and the appearance of the fence in our field of vision was a clear sign that we were on track.

Mother had made sure to have explosives, and a tool box packed so that we could blow a hole in the fence if that's what we needed to do in order to escape. She had never worked with explosives, and the idea of her wiring military grade weapons to a fence frightened me. Mother could be unpredictable at times, and perhaps that is why I thrived on the mundane. I had always enjoyed routine behaviours: getting out of bed at the same time, even on the weekend, doing similar activities on a daily basis, with little variation, the same hiking trails, the same foods at the same times. It had become a compulsion, and I felt upset if my routine was disturbed. Mother's trip broke me of that habit, and a child was the perfect reason to change. "Mom," I called back at her "I think you need to come see this!" I could hear her soft slippers slough against the floor. She placed her hand on my shoulder and braced herself against the passenger seat; we looked ahead at the fence that rose above us. It was a twenty foot high brick fence, with barbed wire coiled along the top. We came to an abrupt stop, and stepped out of the trailer, the hum coming from the fence was low and nauseating. "There's no hope of getting out." My heart fell, and I was ready to crawl back into the trailer and home to the Centre. "Nothing is ever as bleak as it seems, darling. Nor is anything quite what it seems; at least not as far as the Taktikhause is considered." She had picked up a stone, and threw it at the fence. The stone passed through the fence, as though it had been tossed into a lake. Mother pulled her arm into herself in a sort of victory dance "You see." She smirked triumphantly "This is just the beginning. Now," she motioned me to go back to the trailer "Let's get Addie ready; we don't know what it's like out there." She always flopped into the seat with a loud sigh of relief. "My equipment!" I couldn't believe that I had forgotten about it "We should tie it to a rope, send it over, and pull it back once it's had a chance to take readings." Mother smiled at me approvingly "That's my girl! Well, what are you waiting for?"

We used the half hour it would take for the readings to be complete to look at mother's old Atlas, have lunch, and take Addie for a walk. The results came back negative for radiation, and air pollutants, but we could never have prepared for what we would see or feel as we passed through the mirage.

NEW FRONTIERS

The walls of the trailer shook violently, Addie shrieked as if someone had just taken him and thrown him onto hot coals, our skin burned and tightened, our hair stood on end, our muscles tightened; it was pure agony. The minute it took for us to pass through had felt like an eternity of torture. I got up out of my seat and ran back to Addie, our muscles relaxed, and the burning sensation subsided almost immediately. I rocked him gently, and wiped the tears from his cheeks, and brought him up to the front of the trailer.

"My God!" I felt faint "Is this...?" I looked to mother for answers, and found her sitting tears streaming down her face.

"Yes." She looked at us, gently placing her hand on Addie's head "That's Parliament Hill."

It was mid-November, and though the temperature had fallen below freezing, not a speck of snow was to be seen. The ground was barren, dry, and cracked; the bones of thousands of bodies littered the earth around us. "Oh mom." I couldn't imagine how she was feeling at that moment. Her pain must have been insufferable. She took in a deep breath to calm herself and roughly wiped away her tears. "There's no use in just parking here. We need to keep moving. Let's check out the ministerial offices, maybe there'll be something there that we can use, something that can help us." The trailer bounced as we crunched over the bones that littered the streets, some had been picked clean by wildlife, others had decayed slowly, while others seem to have had their clothing, and personal effects stolen. Despite the blue, bright, cloudless sky, the world around us was gray and grim. The sun beamed down a blood red. "We're almost there." Mother was trying to figure out the safest, and quickest way to find what she needed most of all "You'll stay here with Addie; keep a gun close—if the naked skeletons are any indication of sustained life out here, you'll want to protect yourselves." I had never seen her so stern, so focused. "I'll run into the PMO, I'm pretty certain that I can find my way around, and I'll get what I came for." I wasn't certain what she could need from inside the PMO so I asked, but she refused to answer me. I did as she had instructed me to; I sat with Addie in the trailer with the shotgun nearby, mother had taken the Electrobolt—a pistol which shot a bullet that upon contact unravelled into a series of connected wires and electrocuted its target. Addie and I played with his rattles, and ate a jar of peaches, and as I put on the kettle to make a cup of tea, I heard a rustling coming around the sides of the trailer. I grabbed Addie and the shotgun and braced myself against the kitchen counter, as the door flung open and mother stepped in. I put the gun down "Mom!" my knees buckled "You scared the shit out of me!" She bolted the door behind her, and tossed a file box onto the table "Here," she swallowed hard as she tried to catch her breath "You drive, I'll read."

I strapped Addie into his seat at the table, made the tea, and took to the driver's seat. "Where am I going?" I hollered back at her.

"East, just keep driving Eastward." Her gaze was focused in on her files. As I drove away from the Hill, I saw billboards strewn with bodies like tinsel hanging off of a WinterMas tree. Craters from where bombs fell were littered across the landscape, and there was an overwhelming smell of rot that overshadowed the green grass which peaked out from beneath the graveyard. The roads were cracked, and in some places completely missing, making the drive an interesting mix of pavement, dirt, bones, and shrapnel. I couldn't help but imagine her involvement in all of it. We had never been given permission to view the videos in school, we read about them, but the videos themselves had been locked up in a vault. Had she ever pulled the trigger? Did she ever kill anyone? Had she really revealed everything she knew in her memoir? I hoped that one day I would be brave enough to ask her, but I feared I would never have a chance to. I pulled the trailer to a sudden stop. The file box fell, and all of the papers went sliding down the floor "What are you doing!?!" Mother's question was rhetorical, and she went about the business of picking up the papers.

I jumped out of the trailer and ran towards the ditch. "Hello?" I called out as loudly as I could "It's alright, I won't hurt you. I promise." The little girl came out from within the scorched remains of a minivan; her hair was tangled in dreadlocks, her dress was tattered, and made up of patches of old rags, she carried with her a small leather satchel which seemed to be full, and a water skin which was empty. Her face was smudged with blood and dirt. "Hi." I crouched down in a display of friendliness. "Who are you?" Her little voice rang through the field. "I said, who are you?" she grew louder, angrier. "I'm Marie, I come from beyond the fence. What's your name?" She was stealthy, her feet were quick and quiet, as she came closer I could see that she had piercings in her lips and ears. "Maelynne" she walked around me, pinching at my woolen sweater, and scarf. "I live over the ridge, and through the hills. This is my first great journey here. I've come looking for game." She couldn't have been more than ten years old. "What is that?" She pointed at the trailer; mother was standing at the door, holding her gun close and tight. "Oh, that?" I faced the trailer, as I crouched next to her

"That is called a trailer. It is for traveling far. You see, Maelynne? My mother, son and I are on a journey to find something that had been lost to my mother before the Final War." The girl smiled. "To be at war, is to be human." At that she ran off towards the woods across the field. I had a sneaking suspicion that something was about to go terribly wrong. "Get back in mom! I think we need to leave, and quickly!" I looked in the direction that she had run, and saw smoke rising from somewhere along the far edge. I drove as quickly as I could, while swerving to miss the large holes of missing pavement, and tree roots which were beginning to overgrow the road. I feared for our lives. My heart was pounding against my chest, my blood rushed the adrenaline through my veins, and my breathing grew rapid and shallow. Addie was screaming in the back as mother struggled to get him buckled in while he bounced and kicked. I swerved this way and that to avoid large obstacles, but the bumps in the road were unavoidable. "Hold on!" I yelled back at her, and heard the click of Addie's seatbelt locking—there were large pieces of American military bomber jets along the next two kilometer stretch—I pulled right, then a sharp left, swerving in and out, trying to avoid the largest pieces, hoping that the tires would stay intact as we rolled over chunks of metal, wiring, screws, and nails. As we pulled around the last jet we saw a line of men standing across the width of the road, blocking us from moving forward. "What do I do?" I called back to my mother, she didn't answer, and all I could hear was Adalhard screaming, I quickly glanced back and saw mother on the floor under the kitchen table; she must have fallen and hit her head as I swerved to and fro. "Shit, shit, shit, shit, shit!" I was panicking and I didn't know what to do. I pushed down on the accelerator as hard as I could. I wasn't willing to allow my mother, my son and me to become victims to some group of vagabonds. I got closer and closer, and they still wouldn't move out of the way, I fought with myself to keep my foot on the accelerator. I drew closer, so close that I could see their scraggly beards, their thin arms, and emaciated bodies. This was no group of great vagabond warriors; they were nothing like I imagined survivors would be. These were a group of sickly, hungry people trying to survive a world that was unforgiving, and harsh.

I slammed on the brakes, and came to stop just inches from their line. I could see them release a collective breath of relief. I unbuckled, propped Addie on my hip, and placed a small pillow under mother's head. I removed the electrobolt from her side, and held it firmly in my left hand. I stepped out of the trailer. "What do you want?" I yelled at the line of men. "Well, which one of you is in charge here?" An old man stepped out from behind them; he was wrapped in what looked to be a wolf skin, but larger and thicker, he was tall and strong looking. He had not gone without. "Are you the one that caused my little Mae to light the signal? Have you come here from beyond the glow of the great barrier?"

"Yes, and who are you?" I was shaking.

"I am Trove." His attitude was regal, unflinching.

"Very well, Trove. What do you want from us?" I knew that he would want our food, or clean water, he might have even been after some slaves; mother had told me about groups of people that formed after the

Final War broke out. They would give themselves new names, and band together in tribes going around killing whomever would stand in their way. They strangled, cut throats, broke necks, raped; they did whatever they felt they needed to in order to get what they wanted.

"You see," he paced back and forth in front of us "food out here is scarce, the animals have changed, they have grown unafraid of men, and my people are growing hungry. I'm certain you have food in your trailer, clean water, clothes."

"Why would I give you any of it?" I stared at him in disgust. "You obviously haven't gone without; you've grown fat and lazy while your people work day in and day out and hardly get a morsel. I will gladly share some of what we have brought, but not with you." I could see the anger rise in his face, and the pain of injustice shower over the line of men. I looked to them. "Please, come and have supper with me, my son, and my mother this evening. We will set up camp five kilometers from here." I could see just a small flicker of hope in their eyes. "Please, bring your wives and your children too." I knew we would be outnumbered, but that kindness would buy our safety.

"Kent!" Trove called out, and a young boy—he couldn't have been more than fourteen years old—stepped forward hesitantly "You will keep watch over these women, and if you fail to keep them in line, you will suffer the penalty of death by flogging. Am I understood?" He placed his hand on the boys shoulder, pushing all of his weight into him.

"Yes, sir." He was a wiry boy, his muscles were small but well defined, his hair was darkened with grease and dirt, but would have been a nice blonde, his hazel eyes stared at me and burned into my memory. He took hold of the staff that Trove handed to him. "I will make sure they are ready to feast with you."

"No!" I spoke loudly and confidently "Your chieftain is not welcome at my table. He is already fat, but the rest of you look undernourished. Only those who haven't eaten well in the past week may join us." I continued to point the electrobolt at Trove, and it took all of my might to keep my hand steady and still. Trove smirked, his arrogance shined through in that moment "Very well. I will come, but I won't eat."

"How many of your people are there?"

"Twenty eight." He waved his hand and they all turned and walked away, leaving the boy to guard over us.

"You comin'?" I called after him. He ran over, and looked confusedly first at the trailer, then at me. "Hop in, and buckle up." I secured Addie in his seat, and tended to mother's head injury; she was woozy, and uncertain what to do, or how she even ended up on the floor. "Don't worry mom, everything will be just fine, and we'll be on our way before sunset." Mother spent the afternoon icing her head, and taking care of the baby, and I spent it preparing a supper of canned chicken, potato, and vegetable stew.

"So," I hoped to get Kent to tell me what I needed to know about Trove, about their band "how old are you, Kent?"

"Fifteen." It was obvious that conversation wasn't very important to Trove, or to Kent's parents. His speech was slurred and thick.

"I'm twenty-one. The baby, Adalhard, he's only three months old, and my mother, well she's the woman who started the Final War—well, she got things really rolling. My Papa, he worked for the Taktikhause for a long time..."

"What's that?" He had probably never even known that we had established a great nation, let alone how we governed it.

"I'm sorry, ummm, the Taktikhause is a group of men and women who the people of our nation—our tribe—have selected to lead us." It was the only way that I could explain it; it was how I was taught to understand it.

"How do you select them? Do they fight to the death?" his curiosity was true, and his experience screamed at me through his questions.

"No, not at all!" I passed him a cup of tea "Take a seat, please." He sat down. "Usually two or three people, we call them Runners, from each Ward—each section of the country—travel from town to town, telling the people how they plan to make things better, how they will fix the problems that they face. Then, on a specific day every citizen of our nation that is twenty-one or older may go and deposit their decision to the record keepers. The Runner with the most decision points wins the competition and moves to the Centre where they meet with the other Runners who won—we would now call them Service Persons—and they talk about the problems in each Ward, and how they can fix them."

"So no one has to die?" he was confused at the notion of a democratic system.

"Exactly."

"Do all the people get to eat as much as they need?" he was leaning on his knees.

"Well, not always. Some people have more than others, but everyone gets what they earn. This is one of our problems; some of the people have too much, and waste it, but others don't have nearly enough. The people who have the most don't like the idea of sharing what they feel is rightfully theirs. The only way to change that, without having people die, is for the Taktikhause to change the laws—the rules—about how we distribute food."

"You can do that?" He was immersed "We could never stand up to Trove about that. He always takes more than he and his family need, and the rest of us try to divide what's left evenly. But, there's never enough! We always go to bed with our bellies feeling empty."

"I'm sorry." I took his hand in mine, and squeezed reassuringly. "You can change it! You can confront him; you can be the hero that your people need." He pulled away.

"No," he stood up and shook his head vehemently "no, I'm not strong enough. Many have challenged Trove, but none have been able to overthrow him. He is too strong." The horizon came alive with the twinkle of torch light; the day was short and night was coming soon. I was prepared; I knew that I could lift their spirits, perhaps I could even cause enough of a raucous to be able to sneak away unnoticed.

Mother sat at the window of the trailer, watching carefully, with her hand constantly on the shotgun, while trying to keep Addie calm. He was strapped into his seat so that at any moment we would be able to take off. The stew was ready, and the people were ready to eat; the children were ravenous, and their hands and faces were thick with dirt. I put out basins with warm water, soap, and cloths for them to wash up. Their clean, pink skin was freckled, and the children thought it wonderful to feel clean. Young women who hadn't had a chance in years to wash themselves were surprised at the opportunity, and the renewal of a clean face and hands. My heart ached for them, and I wished that I could stay and help them find ways to have these simple pleasures on a daily basis. As they dug into the stew, the steam warming their faces, their expressions changed from desperation to hope. I had prepared a cake for them, with the finest of simulated chocolate, and butter cream icing. As the little ones picked up their slices and took the first bites their eyes widened, and they smiled from ear to ear. They had never had the opportunity to taste anything remotely like chocolate cake. There was laughter, and conversation, and an air of pure joy; just as a large family dinner ought to be. Kent sat in between his parents, his smile was infectious, and happiness beamed from his face.

Trove stomped in along with his wife, and their

children—none of whom were as well fed as he was, but not so poorly off as the others. Fear swept over those sitting at their supper, and some even vacated their seats, insisting that Trove and his family take their portions. I couldn't help myself; I marched over, incensed and ready to change the fate of this group of survivors.

"No!" I yelled at him "Get your ass up! I told you that you are NOT to come here to eat."

The crowd became silent, and watched as I challenged their leader.

"And who are you to tell me what I can or cannot do?" Trove stood up, shoving his wife out of the way—she fell backwards and hit her head on a rock, and she lay motionless—and moved towards me.

"I may not be one of your people, and thank God I'm not! You are a selfish, disgusting, brute of a man! You are nothing without these people, and yet you treat them as if their lives are meaningless!" My fingers tingled, and my heart raced; I was at least an entire foot shorter than him, but that didn't matter, not at that moment. He raised his hand to strike me, I pulled out the electrobolt, and shot. Within moments he lay on the ground, his body seizing until his heart gave out, and he released his final breath. I had killed a man.

The crowd was silent, and then the murmurs began, the whispers, no one was sure what this meant. Trove's wife lay dead with her head bashed against a rock, Trove's body continued to twitch occasionally as the excess electricity tried to find its way out, back into the capable hands of the earth, and the people were left leaderless. Kent stood up, he relayed what I had taught him, how they could work together, bringing their own ideas on how to make things better, and choosing the ideas that sounded like they would be the most efficient, the most beneficial for everyone. They could adopt a socialist system where everyone would get equal share for work of equal value. None of the children would die of hunger, and the women would be heard, respected. He was a strong speaker, and his confidence grew with every cheer. He was young, but he had a clear vision of what his world ought to look like. He was a man of conscience, determination, and charisma. He was what mother had hoped to be, what papa should have been for the Centre and the Wardsmen. He thanked us and gathered his people together to begin the long trek back to their village. I learned later on that they had settled well into this new way of doing things. The elder members who had been too weak to stand up against Trove, helped bring about the change towards democracy and equality. They taught the children to read, write, and do simple math, to think about the best interests of the group rather than their own interests.

We had a lot of driving to do that night to get caught up, but we could leave these people with the knowledge that their existence could become richer, more fulfilling, and more just. That corruption had not yet besieged the hearts of the young, and had not forced them to become completely disillusioned.

FINDING TREASURES

It took us another four days to get to the Great Lakes, we hadn't had the opportunity of running into any other groups of survivors, and we figured that that was best. There was no telling what other tribes had suffered during their life in the wastelands—though the Center would one day learn that it isn't so easy to take the liberty of those who are unwilling to forfeit it, no matter what the promises of comfort and ease my hold. We had narrowly escaped death, or worse, with our encounter with Trove, and it proved to be enough excitement for the two of us, not to mention we were two women on a mission.

Mother drove for the most part, and I spent the time that Adalhard slept writing down details of our trip; everything from our encounter with Trove and his people, to detailed depictions of the decaying landscape. There was little hope in that respect. The land was dry, and barren, what little vegetation grew was strange, and my equipment had a difficult time getting accurate readings; I guessed that the radiation and toxin levels were ever changing in some of the plants. I took some cuttings of the ones which intrigued me the most, but we never stayed for more than a few minutes at a time, for fear of coming across an animal that we couldn't identify, or fight off, or another tribe. The first night we drove was terrifying. We saw eyes glowing for miles on end, and we decided from that moment on that we would take turns driving at night. I would drive from sunset to midnight, and mother would drive from midnight to dusk. She had never slept well, at least not since Parliament Hill. She would wake in cold sweats, sometimes screaming, other times just silently staring at the wall, the guilt and pain written all across her face.

On the third night I pulled over just long enough to stretch my legs, and within moments I heard an eerie howling, as if the wind itself had come from the mouth of a wolf. The ground began to shake in a rhythmic pattern, and as I looked out the window the shadow of a creature came bolting towards us. It looked to be half the size of the trailer, and probably weighed just as much if not more. Its eyes glowed red in the dark night, and the moonlight gleamed off of its razor sharp teeth. I drove off as quickly as I could, hoping that the creature would relent after a short while. It chased us for what felt like hours. I resolved to never stop when driving at night, except when mother and I switched spaces.

Mother woke me when she saw the first glimmer of moonlight off of the water's surface. We pulled over, and stood, staring out at the vast expanse in front of us. The air was cold, and the earth beneath us was brittle with frost, my nose grew cold, and my cheeks reddened quickly. Mother released a sigh of relief, we were close now. She would finally be able to find her answers—had she really been at fault this whole time? Or, was this fate inevitable one way or the other?

It would still take us a few days to drive through to Lake Eerie, but Lake Superior was a great place to start feeling relieved, to allow ourselves some time to enjoy our trip. The sun was ready to rise over the horizon, and it painted the sky into a pastel rainbow of pinks, purples, reds and oranges. The Lake seemed to glow with the sun's rising. "We should spend the day, allow ourselves a little rest." Mother went in to start on breakfast. "It would be a shame if we couldn't tell Addie that he was the only child of his generation to spend a day picnicking at Lake Superior." I could hardly hear her over the sound of the birds waking, and greeting the morning with their songs. It was overwhelming, and couldn't help but imagine a time when lovers would sit on benches, or on the beach under a blanket, waiting for the sun to rise or to set and make the world a beautiful place once more. I took out my equipment, and ran the water through the pocket spectrometer, and found that despite the levels of toxicity that had been recorded even in the early twenty-first century, and despite what the nuclear attacks should have done to the water, it was perfectly safe. This was the only water outside of the Centre and the Wards that could be said to be able to sustain life, yet we could not tell if anyone had been to its shores recently. We spent the day walking the beaches, allowing Addie to experience the texture of sand, how it feels when it gets between your toes, how it flows through your fingers like water, how gritty it is, and how impossible it is to wash off of your body the first time around. He may have been small, and we knew he would never remember it, but at least we could tell him that he touched sand, that he had been witness to the Earth's ability to heal herself when left alone by human hands.

As the sun set we watched the pale blue sky dance with the colours of late fall, and the glimmer of moonlight bounce off of the surface of the water. It didn't take us long to pack up our picnic site, and get back on the road. We took two days to drive East to what had once been Toronto. We stopped along the way, but only during the day when we could see for miles. On the second day of driving we hit a heavy patch of fog; the air was damp and suffocating, it smelled thick with sulfuric acid, and we watched as the beads of fog condensed onto the trailer's hood and slowly started to melt away the paint. So we drove faster, more aggressively, holding onto little hope that we would make it beyond this cloud safely. The roads were rougher than in other areas, and we found ourselves swerving left and right almost constantly to avoid hitting buildings, medians, knocked over signs, posts, and carcasses. As we emerged from the foggy haze what little was left of the Toronto skyline came into our field of vision. Bones, picked clean by scavengers littered the sides of the road, some had nooses loosely wrapped around their necks, others were scattered across miles, cars which had flipped onto their hoods contained the corpses of families; parents who had died on impact with their infants trapped in their car seats to starve or be killed by hungry animals. What had happened to cause so much death and destruction, to cause people to leave crying babies to die? Mother knew, she knew all too well what had happened.

The last bombs had fallen, as far as we knew, when I was only five years old. To me, the mayhem was never apparent, my parents had constructed a home life that kept me innocent of what was happening, but I can recall vividly sitting on the top of the staircase listening to mother weep as she watched the daily news updates. I had thought that perhaps I had done something to disappoint her, but her tears were heavy with guilt. By now the rains had washed away the blood from the grass, and recycled the nutrients from all of the rotting bodies, the wind had swept away the foul stench of decay and returned a fresh breath of new air.

"Please," mother came to the front "stop here. I just need to take a little walk." I pulled over carefully, trying not to crush the bones of some poor, unfortunate soul. I took Adalhard out of his seat and slung him onto my hip and we walked. Mother kept some ten feet ahead of us, and I watched helplessly as her shoulders rose and fell with every sob. She walked towards a minivan, the doors and windows were shut tightly, as she peered in she let go of her breath and fell to her knees. Inside the minivan was a family, one parent was resting atop the standard safety airbag—it looked as though he died quickly—the other adult, who must have been injured badly held onto a small child no older than three years old. The older children had pulled themselves towards their parents—none of them were old enough to be able to walk away from this scene and save their family, so they stayed, huddled up with their family, and resolved to die together. I pulled Addie closer to me, he was hungry and fussing, and I was trying to imagine how it must have felt to tell that baby that there was nothing to eat, to just close its eyes, to surrender to death.

I took mother by the arm, and we walked, slowly, solemnly back to the trailer. We would return another time to bury this family properly. We would find a way to commemorate these lost souls.

Mother knew exactly where we had to go, which streets to turn down, which alleys to navigate through. It never did take her very long to pull herself together, and regain control over her emotions—I had always envied that about her. "How do you do it, mom?" She looked over at me puzzled "How do you calm down so quickly? So, effortlessly?" She chuffed "It took me a long time to learn, but I had to. I've shed far too many tears in my lifetime." She kept driving, focused on the goal, hoping, probably praying that she would find the lock to fit our key.

"Here it is." She whispered it to herself, as she pulled up in front of a store; a simple reassurance that she had remembered where her path and her father's legacy collided. The windows had been smashed in, the shelves were bare, and the hardware was in disarray, the door banged open and shut with the light breeze, and the dank stench of moths and mold filled our lungs. Mother led us up the stairwell, which was heavy with the smell of decay, and down the hall; parts of the building had been blown apart, and there remained gaping holes where there had been apartments, but at the end of the hall, behind a dingy yellowed door lay the rooms in which they had contrived to bring about a change in government: to make things better. The door was partially open; no one had bothered to lock up before leaving. "It's exactly the same," She didn't sound impressed "except that it smells better."

"So," I was directly behind her, stuck in the threshold "what are we looking for?"

She wandered in, picking up pieces of paper that had been left behind "You know, your dad and I never did finish the job."

"What?" I grimaced uninterestedly.

"We were supposed to stop all Oil production, but we never received word that we would have support." She looked around the empty room, empty take out containers, dirty cups and dishes, random articles of clothing left behind by people in a hurry to leave. "Something had to have gone wrong here after Parliament Hill. The bombings started almost immediately, and everyone who was left in this room knew too much." She wandered into the single bedroom. The bedding was disheveled and yellowed over time. There was a small dresser in the corner. Mother went directly to it, and pulled out each drawer. "The bottom-most drawer has a false bottom; we had kept sensitive documents in there." It was empty. We scoured every inch, tipped every drawer, knocked along th e walls, walked around to find loose floorboards. We came up empty handed, well not entirely; mother came across a loose floorboard and found an envelope marked *DANI*. Inside was a brief note: *Keep looking, and remember. "Dzwon, dzwon, dzwon dzwoneczku."* She recognized the code, she knew instinctively where she had to look, and without saying a word turned on her heels, and ran. Addie and I chased after her. She was halfway down the road when she realized she had forgotten us. She backed up, and the *Beep, Beep, Beep*ing of the trailer echoed through the hallowed streets. I hopped in with Addie, unwrapped him and placed him gently into his secure bed for a nap.

"Where are we going?" I plopped down into the passenger's seat.

"Montreal." Her eyes were wide with exhilaration.

The sun was low in the sky, and our stomachs were growling from hunger. I went back to make us an easy to eat supper of sandwiches, to find that our cupboards were growing frighteningly empty. The dinner we had put on for the tribesmen had cost us most of our food, and I hadn't thought of how we would restock. We had packed enough to last us around two weeks, and we had at least another week of travels ahead of us with only three days worth of food.

"Mom," I called up to her

"What is it?"

"Do you think there'll be any useable canned food left in Montreal?" I felt odd asking this about a city that had most likely been decimated.

"Probably not, why?" She looked back at me for only a moment.

The impact sent me flying forwards, the side of mother's head hit the steering wheel, and Adalhard was jostled about—more frightened than harmed. I came to, the sound of my pulse assured me that I was alive, and Addie's crying gave me comfort to know that he survived. "Mom?!?" I pulled myself up onto my knees; the world spun around me. "Mom?!?" I yelled as loudly as I could, but no answer came from her. I stood up carefully; the ground beneath me felt fluid as though I were walking on a tilted trampoline. I felt the trickle of blood come down from my left ear, onto my neck. "Mom?!?" She was unconscious; I lay her down gently, and searched for a pulse, felt for breath. I pushed, and I breathed, and pushed, and breathed, until my lungs hurt, and my arms felt weak. She was gone. There was nothing more that I could do. My mother was gone, the cupboards were nearly empty, I had no idea where to go, or how to get there, and Adalhard; I had forgotten about Adalhard. He had stopped crying.

I stood up, and ran, walked really, as quickly as I could to him. "Addie? Addie baby?" I unbuckled him from the little bed, picked him up, and he squirmed. He had fallen asleep. I checked him over, tested him for a concussion, or even worse injuries; I couldn't lose him and mother on the same day. I wouldn't let anything else go wrong. We stepped out of the trailer to find that we had driven over, with too high a speed, a small piece of airliner debris. The trailer's tires were still intact, there was no other major damage, and we would be able to continue on with our journey. I pulled mother's body out onto the side of the road, and with Addie in my arms I picked a bunch of wild flowers, and placed them in her hands, and in her hair. I covered her body with a blanket; it was the best that I could do.

My hands were numb from the impact and the cold, my ribs were bruised, and my balance was questionable; there was no way that I could dig a proper grave. Truth was that I probably shouldn't have continued on until I had had a chance to regain my balance, but I couldn't give myself over to grief, not when I needed desperately to move forward. I wasn't sure how much further to go, all I knew was that I had to find Montreal. I needed to fix what my mother never could. A task that I understood would be nearly impossible for me to execute.

I drove slowly, cautiously, yet numbly through the rest of the day, stopping often to check on Addie. The sun was low in the sky and I had grown tired and hungry. I pulled over, took Addie out of his seat, breathing in his sweet musk; there is nothing quite like the sweetness of a baby's scent. I sat, watching him try to roll over from his stomach onto his back, his legs kicking furiously, his head bobbing, the bald spot on the back of his perfectly round little head had worn itself in. We stepped out for a quick walk, the landscape around us was speckled with the glow of fireflies, and I thought it strange that there should be fireflies at this time of year. The ground beneath my feet groaned and rumbled, and the glow changed from a calming twinkle to a raging swarm. I didn't bother putting Addie back in his seat, I held him tightly and sped off, praying, begging for a miracle. I drove that way for hours. By the time my heart had slowed, the moon was high in the sky—it must have been nearing midnight—so I stopped, there was no sign of life as far as I could see. I fed and changed Addie and laid him gently down to sleep for the night. I was wide awake, and had no hope of the adrenaline fading away any time soon. I was too afraid to slow down, and too tired to cry, so I just drove as long and as far as I could.

My mind wandered to quiet nights spent curled up on the chesterfield, a glass of wine, a fire roaring in the fireplace, and a good book to flip through. I imagined myself back home, quietly creeping out of the nursery—one that I had yet to plan—gently shutting the door, and pouring a hot bath for myself while my favourite record played off in the distance. I felt the warmth and softness of my bed, I smelled the lavender candles on my bedside, and knew that it was a mirage, that my mind was wandering to keep me from the reality of being stuck out in the wastelands with no way to communicate with my friends and family at home. I was stranded with a baby. I didn't even know what I was looking for, or why I was looking for it, all that I knew was that it was important to my mother to find it, because she needed some form of closure for failing her father, or perhaps he had failed her. I remembered her scent, the way that her perfume lingered in the air even after she had left the room, but she had never worn too much. Memories of her cooking breakfast in an oversized tee and pair of short shorts, her hair tossed up into a quick bun, her mascara smeared from going to bed without washing her face. Her laugh had always resonated and was often the topic of discussion, at least for a few moments after she had laughed. Her laughter was always genuine, she had never bothered with faking anything. If she was going to make a claim that she baked something, she made sure that she made it from a recipe in a book, not from the back of a box. There were flashes of her dancing around the house, using a wooden spoon as a microphone, and the pain of knowing that as soon as I went to bed she and papa would argue about politics, and what to do about it.

    When I realized how far we had come, all while

in a trance of remembrance, I saw the pink grapefruit sky melting into a yellow sun bursting from the ice blue waters of what had been the St. Lawrence River. The bent and worn road sign showed that Montreal was only a couple of hours away. Mother and Papa had made Montreal sound like the most amazing place to live; as though the city had sparkled with culture. My head spun, and my stomach ached with hunger, my mouth was sticky and dry with thirst, and I became acutely aware of the time that had passed. I had taken care of the boy's needs, but not my own, out of some twisted sense of justice for her death. It hadn't been my fault, but I felt responsible. He stirred and grunted as I walked back to take him out of his bed. "So, baby" I spoke quietly to him "Should we take the day so that mama can get some rest?" I lifted him up into the air "I think so!" I started changing him "And while we play, mama is going to tell you all about your Babcia, all about how beautiful she was, and how kind, and how she made the world change." We ate our breakfast, a bottle of simulated breast milk for Addie, and a cup of oats for me—I had begun to lose weight, and my clothes were growing too big for my body since our encounter with Trove's people. I had always been fit, even though some of my friends had always considered me to be a bit "thick". I had never appreciated the standard of beauty that some of them had held themselves to, often going without food for two days before a big event so that they could fit into a dress that was too small. All I had ever wanted for my body was health; I loved the taste, texture, and smell of food, and my legs were built for climbing, dancing, and running. I had never wanted to be frail, helpless, like so many of them—I pitied them, and they knew it. It was one of the reasons why I had few friends to begin with. Mother had always insisted that we eat plenty, and move our bodies often; she rarely sat in one spot for very long. She would tell me that you had to be strong to change the world, that chains couldn't be broken by someone who was weak, that our bodies showed the outside world what kind of person we are on the inside. The rest of the day had gone by uneventfully, we walked for a little while, rested, and by the time the light had started to fade I was ready to move forward. I wasn't certain what I had expected to see as the Montreal skyline rose ahead of me. I suppose I had wanted the streets to be clear of debris and bodies, the roads to be repaired as though nothing had happened there, but the reality was as grim as when we had found ourselves manoeuvring around carcasses in Toronto. The highway was littered with bodies, shrapnel could be found sticking out of the earth, covered in moss and vines. The earth had made use of the debris that had been left behind. The soil looked fertile, perhaps the plants had adapted, and the animals seemed eager to eat. As we drove through I could see rabbits, and deer grazing. Their ears perked up at the sound of the engine, one that these generations would not understand, it was new to them. As we pulled through the suburbs, houses falling apart with overgrown lawns that began to stretch out into the street, the silence was only broken by the sound of birds, and the gentle hum of the engine. As the sun began to set over the rooftops, the sky turned an ominous purple; the kind that sets into a bruise after a day or two. It reminded me that the earth was still hurting, that the damage that seemed so distant from my comfortable life, was still very real, and that the world was only beginning to heal itself. Mother had once told me that just before the bombings had started, scientists had predicted a complete loss of arctic ice within five years, and still governments and industry wouldn't change their practices. It would have proven to be a losing battle.

I had always wanted to go to the Arctic, see for myself if the ice was still there, if it had completely melted away, or if it had had the chance it needed to begin recuperating. Dusk began to settle onto the rooftops and it was becoming difficult to see. I could barely make out the shape of the woman walking down the middle of the road in the glow of the headlights, but as she came closer I could make out her frailty. I stopped the trailer, took Addie and placed the electrorad in its holster on my hip. As we stepped out I could tell that there was a determination in her steps. "Hello?" I hollered at her, she must have been some twenty feet away, and didn't respond. "Hello?" I tried again. She was close enough to see clearly now, and stopped suddenly.

Her skin was dark, the colour of chestnuts, her auburn hair was cut short, and her clothes were a mix of animal skins and cloth that she had probably cut off of dead bodies, or pillaged from a skeleton's closet. She was barefoot and unarmed. "My name is Marie, this is my son, Adalhard; I call him Addie." I approached her cautiously. "What's your name?" We were within stone's throw, and I was no longer yelling to her. She looked at me curiously, like a bird on the promenade that wonders if you've brought bread in your pocket. "Callie." Her voice was meek, but thick and held in it the promise of a powerful song. "That's a beautiful name." I came just a little bit closer; she didn't flinch. "What do you want?" She was demanding in her stance, and her accent was a mix of Papa's Quebecois and the Newfoundland mumble that some of mother's closest friends carried on in. "We're just trying to get to McGill University's bell tower; my grandfather left something there years ago, and I've come to collect it." I tried to be assertive and non-threatening, but my voice shook, and my arms grew tired of holding Addie close.

She glanced us over, and as her eyes reached

the tops of my shoulders she looked beyond us at the trailer. Her eyes narrowed, her brow furrowed, and her countenance grew concerned and uncertain. She straightened her back, and pulled her shoulders further behind her, as if she were posturing for a fight. Her feet moved swiftly, silently underneath her as she circled around us and stalked towards the trailer. "It's perfectly safe!" I called out as we sped by. "All that's in there is some food, clothes, a restroom, kitchen, and a bed." I had climbed back inside, I leaned out the door, "You're welcome to come in and take a look for yourself." Friendliness was the only way I could see out of this situation. Her hand slowly took hold of the wooden railing—mother had complained that it looked like something out of the nineteen-seventies—and her right foot pushed itself firmly into the first step, her movement was tentative.

"Is this where you live?" She looked around, puzzled.

"Well, just while we're on the road." I placed Addie in his seat, buckled him in, watching her through the mirror.

"What do you mean? Where do you come from?" Her gaze burrowed through me.

"I've come from the West, from The Centre. It used to be called Banff before the bombings, but they re-named it The Centre because that's where everyone accumulated, and it really did become the centre of everyone's existence and hope for survival." I worked hard at being nonchalant.

"That's where my uncle said that my parents were heading, to Banff, when mother went into labour a few miles outside of Montreal. Then when mother died from infection after having me in the aftermath of a nuclear strike, my father decided that he had to see if there were any other nursing mothers that he could ask to help keep me alive. So, when he found Madame Brigeux with her six kids, he knew that so long as she could feed me, that we would have to stay with her. Madame was a stubborn cow, he would say, and my father eventually fell in love with the woman who so selflessly gave her milk for me. So we stayed behind, because his love refused to leave her home." She plopped down into a kitchen chair.

"So, you've lived here your entire life?" It seemed impossible to me after everything that we had been taught in school about the wastelands, about how dangerous, unpredictable, and uninhabitable they were.

"Yes." She placed her elbows on her thighs and placed her chin in her hands, "So, tell me about this Centre. Are there many people? Are they nice? Do you hunt and gather? How is labour divided among your people?"

Her eagerness to learn was striking and unexpected.

"There are millions of people now, many of them, obviously, migrated from all across the Americas—North, Central, South—to seek refuge as they began to hear of the settlement and safety there. Some of them were sent out to work camps, which we've now given borders, local governments, and so forth, to as the populations grew. These camps turned into towns, and have expanded so that we've called them wards. People aren't allowed to travel between wards unless they have special permission; it keeps everyone safe." I poured tea into cups and warmed a bottle for Addie.

"So, you aren't free there." She seemed certain that what she had was freedom, and what we had was bondage.

"No, of course we're free! The thing is, when you have such a large population, and you have to divide the resources among all of the people, divide labour, and protect people from one another, the government has to set guidelines for behaviour, and enforce them. These rules that we have, they are for our protection. The world outside of our borders is dangerous, every ward has its own customs, and if one isn't careful about minding those customs, well, let's just say that sometimes people can get very upset about that." The more I defended the laws, and the more vehemently I stood up for these ideals, the more I realized how much of a slave to the Taktikhause I was. She told me about how simple life could be out here, how she spent her days walking, watching the animals to see where the ground was safe to eat from—she was convinced that they could sense the poison from the irradiated earth in the plants. Animals have always been more intuitive than us, they've always been closer to the earth, they have always been better equipped to sense changes in climate well before they ever happened. This girl fascinated me; her understanding of how the world operates, of science, without any formal education was astounding.

"We should get going." She took in a deep breath and looked through the window. "We won't be safe out here for very long." She began to head for the door.

"Why don't I just drive to wherever you want us to go." I couldn't risk having Addie out in the air if it wasn't going to be safe. "It'll take less time."

The house would have been beautiful when it had first been built. The remnants of white paint peeled from the siding, and the shingles on the roof were missing in places, and curled in others. The windows were boarded up to keep out whatever it was that made the night dangerous. The steps leading up to the house had become overgrown with weeds, and the lawn was a mixture of wild flowers, and vegetables.

"Quickly, quickly!" An old woman waved at us

from the front door. Her gaze was fixed to the East where the fog was beginning to pour in. The wind had picked up from a slight breeze to a steady, almost mechanical blowing. Callie ran into the house, and I followed suit with Addie hanging off of my hip. The old woman shut the door, locked it, and quickly filled the cracks with rags. "Jesse." She looked up at me from her crouched position at the door, and extended her right hand. "Marie." I pulled her up "and this is Adalhard." Her expression was stern, displeased at our presence. Callie ushered us to the sofa, and went to the kitchen with Jesse. Callie returned after a few minutes of having to explain herself. "I'll show you to your room. Supper will be ready soon, so wash up and come straight down. They have some questions for you." She turned on her heals and headed up the stairs. Our room was at the end of the hallway. It had been a nursery, there was a crib, and a twin bed. The walls had been painted a pale pink, but had yellowed over the years, and the carpet would have once been a soft beige. The bedding was tattered and stitched repeatedly over the years, and had become a mixture of blankets, and sheets from different peoples' houses. I put our things in the corner, changed Addie, and went down to supper.

"So," an elderly man stood up from his seat at the table "Our girl says that you're from the West, from the settlement."

"Yes." One word answers were my safest option.

"And this is your boy?" Another voice, younger, but by only a decade, came out from behind the counter.

"Yes, he's mine."

"He's a little dark to be yours." The old man had sat down, and motioned for me to sit.

"He's adopted." My heart raced, and my palms sweated.

"Tell us about the settlement." Their attention was on me, and I told them everything they could have needed to know. Technology, politics, population, safety, laws. All of it, even about the laws that would have meant Addie's death if not for mother's quick thinking.

"Impressive." The smell of freshly cooked meat

filled the room. "Now, let's say grace, and you can tell us what brings you out here." The old man lead the prayer, and everyone seemed to wait for him to take the first bite. I told them about my parents, about my dziadek's journals, and mother's mission to find what he had left for her, and how Montreal was the only place that she could think to go. They agreed to help me get to McGill, to keep me and Addie as safe as possible, so long as I could help them get west. I promised them I would. When supper was finished, and everyone retired to their beds, Callie came up with a pot of fresh herbal tea "You mentioned on the way here that you weren't sleeping well. This should help." She stood in the door for a moment "Don't be upset with Amos, he's old, and, well, he's rather overprotective of me."

"I'm not, and thank you." It was too hot, and it burned my throat as I swallowed. My bed was lumpy, and the blanket was thin, but I was grateful for their help. For the first time since mother's death I was able to close my eyes, and allow myself to cry. The trip would be over soon, and I would be able to get back to my life in the mountains. I would teach

Addie about which berries are safe to pick, which mushrooms were poisonous, and how to scale mountains. There was a glimmer of hope for a quiet life, the kind that my papa always dreamt of.

Morning came too soon, and the tears had collected in the corners of my eyes; Addie was laying on his blanket, making cooing sounds as the spit that he wouldn't swallow bubbled around his lips making them shine. The light peaked in from underneath the door—the sun was still hiding beyond the horizon—and whispers traveled up the stairs from the kitchen carrying with them the smells of sausages and eggs. "Mmmmm" I stretched out my body, wiggling my toes, "Doesn't that smell good, Addie? They must have a chicken somewhere, or maybe they've caught some other birdies to lay their eggs." I picked him up, and gently blew on his face—I loved how he would hold his breath, just for a moment. When we were dressed, I packed our bag and went down to breakfast. Everyone was silent while we ate, there were no "morning people" to be found in this bunch.

The day was new, and our company was eager

to help us on our way. They had never thought that anyone would travel towards the wastelands, so their curiosity pushed them to move faster than they normally would. I was surprised that old Amos was able to keep up; his obscured vision and bowed legs didn't prevent him from coming along. "You need me. Callie doesn't know the campus like I do. I taught there for many years." His voice was raspy, and his breath was shallow. "In fact I knew your father. His relationship with your mother had always teetered on the inappropriate, but no one could ever prove that it was anything more than a great friendship." He sneered with disapproval "But I always knew better." His gaze burned into my back. He had ulterior motives, even if Callie had simply wanted to help, or perhaps she knew this would happen, perhaps there was something more sinister about that quiet voice. As we turned the corner I could see the peaks and domes of some of the buildings; even from our distance we were able to make out the impact points. "It isn't a comforting sight," Callie peered back at me "It was where the mass suicides started; students, faculty, children." She looked down at her feet, closing her eyes "we simply can't bury them all."

It didn't take us long to arrive at the bell tower. I left my guides below, and climbed carefully, watching for structural problems, but the tower seemed to have been more affected by age and neglect, rather than by trauma. I didn't know what I was looking for at the top of that tower, but I prayed that the key I wore around my neck would open up something, something that would give me answers to questions that I didn't have. I pushed the warped door that led to the bell and pulleys, open, half expecting something or someone to jump out from behind the bell announcing my victory, but all that stood in front of us was a cracked bell, and frayed and tangled ropes. In the corner, covered in a thick, sticky layer of dust, was a leather bound journal, just like the ones mother had recovered from dziadek's study. This one had a small lock on it, like those on a girl's diary. I took my handkerchief and wiped the dust off, gently; mother had always warned me to be kind to old books, to not sully them with my rough fingers. She described old books as butterfly wings—beautiful, magical, but fragile. The slightest bit of moisture renders the butterfly immobile, just as the smallest smudge of oil from a finger can begin the disintegration of a page. I wrapped the journal, carefully, and placed it in my pack—Addie and I could begin our journey home.

RETURNING

It took us only a day to get Callie's family packed for the trip back. Jesse pulled as much of the fresh vegetables as she thought would be necessary for the journey, and we packed the entire family into the trailer. It was crowded with the eight of us, and since none of them had driven since the bombings, I was left to drive the entire way. We took our time, giving them the opportunity to get to know the new landscape, to grieve for the millions of bodies that littered the roads. We had enough food to last a week. Callie could hardly contain her excitement, and carsickness. I shared with them my experience with Trove, we stopped to give mother a proper burial, and to take in the majesty of the Great Lakes. The push through the magnetic wall was just as painful as the first time. As we approached the first checkpoint, I saw the smoke billowing for miles, black with the stench of flesh and lacquer. I pulled over, prepared our papers, ready to get past the gates; to get back to my quiet life. The toll booth was surrounded by armed guards, and a barbed wire fence had been erected. "Papers!" the guard demanded, his pointed features were accented by his frustration and fear. "Yes, of course." I pretended to shuffle around my purse "Ah, here they are."

"There are only two sets of papers here, and there are eight heads. Explain."

"I went beyond the electric barrier, and I found them. I'm bringing them back to be studied at the Centre." He turned away from me, swiping through the holoscreen; I could see he was confused. "The records state that you are to be stationed at research station fifteen. You don't have permission to go beyond the final barrier." My mind raced to find a suitable purpose "I," I took a long breath "I haven't been able to communicate my findings with base, and I have some very time sensitive samples that I need to take back to the main lab. Now, let us pass!"

He spoke into his wrist, putting forward the request to his supervisor. "Yes, sir." His eyes met mine, they were deep green like the waters of the remaining glacial lakes "You're to report to the Captain; he's curious about your samples. You'll also need a diagnostic before moving further inland." The gate lifted, I thanked the young man, we proceeded straight to the police tents that had been set up. The canvas was worn and smeared by rain and dirt. The protocol was always to set the captain's tent at the centre of the tent city, so we walked with resolve straight in. The captain was a tall man, his hands rolled into fists pushed the entirety of his weight into the table in the centre of the tent. There was a thin cot with a light blanket in the back left corner, and a small night table with a picture frame and a small black book. I stood silently at his door, there was a familiarity in his defeat, and a heaviness in his voice. "Why are you here?" He wouldn't turn around. I was shocked to hear his voice, the voice of a man I was certain had met his end, a man whom I begged to follow me. "I found what I needed." My steps were slow, cautious, with Addie sleeping in my arms, "I thought..."

"I know what you thought." He turned around to face me. His face was scarred from the flames that engulfed his home as we had driven off desperately. "I had hoped you would stay out there. Did you find it?" His steps were heavy, desperate.

"Find what?" I stepped back from him "Did you know what my mother and I were after?" My brow furrowed, I grew angry and frustrated. His body was close to mine, the only space between us was created by Addie, who released a grunt as the tension built. His hand reached out to my cheek, "It's what we've been waiting out here for, for the past ten years."

"Then why?" I allowed my voice to grow, to fill the space around us "Why in the world didn't any of you go after it?"

He scoffed "Because, it was written for your mother, not for us. We wouldn't be able to decipher his hidden agenda." It was so obvious to him it made me sick.

"Well, I'm sorry to disappoint you, but my mother is dead. She died when we sped over some debris from an airplane." The disappointment grew in his eyes. His defeat was made permanent in that moment.

"Who are those people you brought with you?" His tone was accusatory. "Just some survivors who have been too afraid to travel by foot here. I promised to take them to the Centre; I gave them hope for a better life." He waved his hand towards the door "Good. You should get back to your precious little Centre; to your life of ignorance and plenty. You couldn't possibly understand what we're fighting for."

"Whatever." I moved purposefully towards the door.

"Just promise me one thing." He turned from me and slowly moved towards his table "Don't let anyone else study that journal. There are others who worked closely with your mother that understand his scribblings." I left him without saying a word. He had used me, he had gotten my trust, my mother's trust, and if she had survived, he would have exploited it. He still wore the official uniform, and worked under the provision of the Centre, but his motives were to destroy the Taktikhause.

"What's going on?" Callie begged. "Just a little civil unrest is all. We'll need to try and drive non-stop until we get there, it just isn't safe to stop anywhere." We piled in, and the mood changed from hopeful, jovial, to fearful and tense. As we drove into the ward, we came upon the piles of burning bodies that were releasing the thick, black smoke. The ditch was littered with burnt remnants of people's lives, and the scattered throngs that had decided to move west, in hope of finding safety. Children sat, forlorn next to the bodies of their dead parents, every once in a while, a kind neighbour would take the hand of one or two, and guide them gently away from the rotting corpse. Tent cities were few and far between, and were reserved for the armed guard; checkpoints between wards were heavily guarded, but gave us no trouble. Joey must have altered the status of my pass.

As we drove into more neutral ground there was a notable increase in tent cities, these were different, these cities contained refugees—people who hated the Taktikhause for its oppression, but couldn't risk staying in the outlying wards, where the fighting was constant and intense. They were afraid. The agricultural ward had the largest population of these nomads, and the least fighting. The fishery ward, and logging wards were well treated, and so sided with the Centre; they remained loyal throughout the spread of uprisings. Callie's family decided that they wanted to go where they would find some measure of peace, and having originated from Newfoundland, the Taktikhause saw it fit to place them in the fisheries, and allowed Callie to stay in The Centre in order to study. She chose History, and quickly became a favourite of her professors, and of the politicians. She had a quick and tactful tongue, and her mixed accent was soothing, yet stern. She went on to make a good career out of Politics, telling citizens that their concerns were heard, that an action plan was being developed, all while begging me, pleading with me to hand over and translate the notebook.

The Centre squashed small riots quickly and swiftly, with few casualties—the threat of hovering bombers, and hundreds of guns was enough to send most protestors home—but a group of rebels remained, traveling from township to township claiming them as liberated, but all that happened was the removal of services, food, and support. They went on like this for almost two years. Two years that the wards went without their rations, without any freedom, with armed guards at every junction, knocking on each door to ensure that the people observed a strict 7 pm curfew. Once the refugee tent cities were dismantled, and the families sent back to their home wards, it didn't take long for citizens to rise up against the rebel forces and destroy them. Those fights were the ones that led to the most blood-shed, the most broken hearts. The only stipulation the Taktikhause had was that the rebel officers were to be returned to the Centre to be given a proper trial. So, they were arrested, tortured and transported to the Centre for sentencing, which almost always resulted in a public death. Joey's was the most horrific. Perhaps it was because he had been a Peace Officer, employed and trained by the Central government, and he used his knowledge to push the rebellion to a state that became nearly irreversible that he was sentenced to suffer public torture, given nothing but water for a week, his cuts were left to fester and become infected, and only when he begged for death was he released from his chains and made to give a public apology and confession. Every screen in the Centre and in the wards was automatically turned on, and his confession was broadcast live. His body was fragile, weak. He stood in nothing but his soiled underwear with the General and President towering over him in their perfectly pressed suits.

"I have betrayed my country, my family" his tongue was so thick with infection that the words were barely audible "I confess to having conspired against and instigating acts of war and terrorism against the Central government, which has done nothing but protect the interests of its citizens" his eyes were swollen shut, and puss and blood seeped from his wounds "and I offer my most heartfelt, and sincere regrets. Please, forgive..." Before he could finish the General shot him in the side of the head. The screens went black, and cheers began to rise in the streets. People in the Centre were glad he was killed, that he died with absolutely no dignity. I was horrified.

I took all of my samples to the lab, where I was greeted emphatically and celebrated for my adventurous spirit. Addie and I spent a few weeks in and out of the IRC getting tested for radiation, new illnesses, and who knows what else. The tests seemed excessive to me, but that was the benefit of living in the Center and being one of its most revered citizens. After the trials, and the tests, when the wards had settled down back into their routines, and after I had given my testimony of the events that conspired between my leave from the Centre until my return for the fifth time I packed Addie and myself, and moved out to my parent's home. I spent every extra cent I had to help make the lives of the others more bearable. Papa and I would work together to educate the children, and prepare meals for their families, and when it was his time, I kept Addie home, and refused to place him in the state school. I taught him everything that the curriculum demanded, and made him acutely aware of the politics. We were given a stipend from the Centre for our bravery and ability to escape and survive in the wastelands, for the samples that I obtained, which would allow them to push the fence further East and begin exploring areas suitable for vacationing citizens, such as the Great Lakes. It was at this time that I became reunited with Kent. The Taktikhause had asked if there were any survivors that could lead them, give them some inkling of how to navigate the land safely, which flora and fauna were safe for food, which plants had mutated into dangerous strains—these would be gathered, studied, and in time exterminated—and what other unknown dangers lurked in the night. Houses were build up in gated communities along the lakes and the gates electrified to keep out unwanted creatures. Kent regaled us with stories of his people, of how the children were growing strong, of how they would listen to the elders and began to farm crops and raise small animals for their food, and had taken over what had once been a small farming town. He asked me to come and visit them, but I was never able to leave, not because I had made promises to the Taktikhause, but because travel bore too many difficult memories. Addie had the heart of an adventurer. He left me on his twenty-first birthday in search of something to define him. I never heard from him again, but imagined that he would spend his life wandering; exploring areas considered untouchable, unsafe.

ACKNOWLEDGEMENTS

To my Parents for always believing in me, and helping me at every crossroads. My husband, without whom all of the sleepless nights, the crazed moments of inspiration, and the need to work would have been for naught. To my friends who read through my manuscripts and helped me find my errors: Thank you.

ABOUT THE AUTHOR

Marta Jespersen is a stay at home mom, who has always been passionate about literature. Her inspirations are many, and she has always desired to share her literary vision with others. As a child, she and her family immigrated to Canada from Poland, and she has had the exquisite privilege of growing up in two worlds, experiencing two cultures simultaneously. She allows her experiences to bleed into her work, informing the history of her characters, and shedding light on the dark corners of literary truth.

Made in the USA
Charleston, SC
12 November 2014